INEVITABLE

By Mason Hawley Ballowe

Thank you to my friends and family who listened to me ramble about time travel crap.

Thank you to my editors: Jimmy Ballowe, Michael Garrett, Lin Qiu, John Koenig, and Bonnie Schiffman. They did not agree to be named.

Sorry for my descriptions of clothing. I wore 50 hues of blue in my day, Go Air Force, intermixed with camo. Coming up with 500+ years of futuristic fashion is a task I am ill equipped to tackle.

Mostly.

George McFly, thanks for the inspiration.

Chapter 1

March 4, 2015. Washington, D.C.

He glanced down at his trembling hands. He smiled slyly, contorting the right half of his face as he rubbed them against the barrel of his weapon in an attempt to regain his composure. It didn't matter how many missions he went on. Will always felt the fear. It started with unease as he boarded the vessel and only built until the action started. Once it began, Will never faltered. Training kicked in, and he executed. Even after all these years, he couldn't shake the fear.

Will closed his eyes and took a deep breath, slowly exhaling through his nose. The air smelled stale but thick with sweat from so many bodies pushed into the small metal interior of the S.W.A.T. vehicle. He opened his eyes and licked his lips, tasting his own salty sweat. The tension in the carrier was only heightened by the wailing siren as the screech penetrated the metal of the vehicle, and the silence of the team.

Will glanced around the back of the transport. Each of his teammates sat along the benches bolted to the sides. Each man was dealing with fear in his own way. To his right, Harrison was nervously tapping his heels on the ground as he clasped his twelve gauge shotgun between his legs. Both hands gripped the barrel as he looked down at his feet. Will laughed to himself, wondering if Harrison's knuckles were white underneath the black fingerless gloves he wore.

Gazing farther down the line, he saw a row of black combat boots ending in neatly bloused black battle dress pants. Each team member carried different articles into a mission. Some had bulging cargo pockets at their hips, while others kept it light. Will subconsciously reached down to the side of his right thigh and checked his pocket. His towel was still there, even though he had just checked it a few minutes prior. He always went into a mission with his Nats towel. He knew Harrison always kept just a protein bar.

Lifting his eyes to the line of seated officers in the back of the carrier, he nodded confidently at their preparations. Black long sleeve shirts protruded from underneath heavy bullet proof vests. The bold white word "POLICE" stood out in stark contrast to the black of their uniforms. Shotgun shells, grenades of all types, knives, and other assorted ammunition adorned each team member's chest. They were ready.

Will and the rest of the team leaned to the right as the vehicle turned. The turn lasted longer than normal, causing a few members to reach down and push back against the bench. Probably Dupont Circle, Will thought. We must be getting close.

Will straightened himself as the forces stabilized. To his immediate left sat his overwatch. Gabriel, or Roach, as they all called him, gripped his sniper rifle.

Roach could get an overwatch anywhere without being detected. Will always felt safer knowing Gabe had his back. Long dirty brown dreadlocks streamed back from underneath his helmet. Dark olive skin revealed his latin heritage.

Will let his hand slide to his sidearm and back to his cargo pocket, checking each piece of gear to ensure it was still where he'd placed it only moments ago. His hand trembled slightly as his exposed fingers moved against the tough military grade fabric of his uniform.

Glancing straight ahead, he looked at his teammate sitting across from him. Prescott was one cocky son of a bitch. He was armed to the teeth. He carried two side-arms, a knife, a sawed off shotgun with pistol grip over his back, and a rifle clasped casually in one hand, butt against the floor.

Prescott, the guy everyone wanted on their team. He always took point. They all joked he was descended from a Cherokee tracker, even though he was completely white, simply because he could always detect a threat before it was too late. Will looked up into the mirrored lense of Prescott's glasses. Prescott always wore the same aviator style glasses under his helmet. You never knew where he was looking, even when he was staring you down.

Will saw himself, an athletic 6'2" tall man weighing one hundred and ninety pounds. A few back up pistol magazines and M4 magazines were strapped to his chest atop the "POLICE" logo. He looked himself in the eyes through Prescott's lense. He could see the fear and confidence battling for his own composure. He reached up and rubbed his face, feeling the rough stubble rub against his fingers protruding from his fingerless black gloves.

He smiled inwardly at his reddish stubble adorning his face. He hadn't been clean shaven since he separated from the Air Force in 2012. Three years had gone by fast, he thought to himself.

Sergeant Hess, a short black man with a shaved head, rose from his seat in the back to get everyone ready. He grabbed the railings of the upper gear racks and turned to face the team. The blare of the siren, continuous in its annoyance, drowned out the Sergeant's shouts from the back. Will already knew the situation from the pre-brief, shots fired inside an upscale Dupont restaurant called "Mission," unknown number of assailants, unknown number of wounded. Probable hostage, Senator Marcus Shaw of South Carolina. Officer down.

Will leaned right as he felt the vehicle screech to a sudden stop. "GO TIME!" bellowed Sergeant Hess. "On your feet, get your gear, and let's go." Everyone quickly stood, and checked their equipment. Bright sunlight burst into the back of the dark carrier as the door flew open. A loud crash of metal sounded as the metal door impacted the carrier. A blast of winter air pushed through the vehicle, changing tremors of fear to those of cold. Will pulled up his face mask, stepped out of the carrier and into the brutal D.C. chill. Snow and ice crunched under his combat boots as he jumped down to the hard concrete of the street.

Snow fell gently everywhere as the small flurry passed through the city. The tranquility of the winter flurry was cancelled by the tension Will felt in his belly. His vision was fuzzy, and his heart pounded in his chest. The police had set up a perimeter. All weapons were aimed at a nondescript white rowhouse with a thin black wrought iron gate. Red and blue lights flashed from all directions.

At the entrance, large puddles of blood were slowly freezing. The red blood made a stark contrast to the white snow, fresh on the sidewalk. From the biggest puddle of blood, two solid trails and several footprints led away to the police perimeter. Someone had bravely dragged the downed officer away. Small blood spots stained the snow between the two trails. Will already knew the outcome. The downed officer had died en route to the hospital.

The team grouped up on the right side of the transport, shielding their bodies from the cold wind while Sergeant Hess walked over to get an updated status. Roach and the other three members of the sniper team jogged across the street to set up. They'd be heading to the roof to create the overwatch. The rest of the team, eight strong, stood waiting for Sergeant Hess to return. Will looked at Prescott, standing impassively, reflective glasses and stoic demeanor betraying no fear. His rifle was held lazily by his right elbow, aimed at the ground.

Three loud shots rang out from inside the eatery. Everyone ducked, except Prescott. Will looked to Sergeant Hess. He walked back to the team, unphased.

"That's our cue," Sergeant Hess stated tensely. He tapped the microphone toggle on his belt. "Overwatch, do you read me?"

...

"Roach, come in."

...

"We hear you Sarge, what's the word?" Gabe's voice asked over the radio.

"Are you in position? We need to go in ASAP."

"We're in place," came Roach's reply.

"Okay, listen up. Sporadic gunfire has been heard from the building since it all began fifteen minutes ago. We're going in, and we're going in blind. No restrictions on use of force. Estimates are two heavily armed terrorists. They've already killed at least one cop, and who knows how many hostages. We also estimate at least twenty hostages, and Senator Shaw is confirmed inside, although we don't know his status. Take these fuckers down, save the hostages, save the senator," Sergeant Hess ordered.

"Inside is a three story establishment. The ground floor is an open space and a bar on the left. Keep at eye on it at all times until cleared. Seating areas are to the right, kitchen in the back. The kitchen has a solid wall divider. It's connected to another large seating area leading from the bar area, kitchen, and back door. It'll likely have lots of heavy equipment and places to hide. Be careful. Check your corners. There is a spiral stairwell in the kitchen, and full staircase in the hallway at the back of the seating area.

"The second floor is an entirely open seating area with a small server station and bathrooms. The third floor is storage only. Lots of small rooms, possible hostages holed up inside. We have to clear floor by floor. Remember, two is just a rough estimate. Honestly, we have no fucking idea what's going on inside. The initial responding officer is the only one to make contact, and he was shot repeatedly as soon as he approached the door.

"Bravo team is Harrison, Jos, and Flory. Head around back and enter through the rear entrance, second floor. Alpha team is Prescott, Will, and Mike. Front door, ground floor. Move."

All six men hoisted their weapons, checked their

gear one last time, and began walking down the street away from Mission. After one hundred feet, Alpha team crossed, and turned to face their target. As they waited for Bravo team, they stood close to the wall of a faded pink home in the row of houses.

Will watched as Bravo team trudged farther down the block. Black boots making small imprints in the shallow white snow. The three men reached the corner of the nearest alley, turned, and headed to the rear of the buildings.

"It's almost time. Ya'll ready?" Will asked his team. Two heads bobbed in return.

The three men stood in silence. Mike nervously checked each piece of gear one final time to ensure it was there. He pulled a wadded roll of condoms from a cargo pocket and grinned. "Let's wrap it up in here quickly, then wrap it up across the street. I'm sure there's a congressman's neglected side chick looking to make someone jealous. I hope to be that mistake." He shook his head at the lack of reaction, still smiling unabashedly. He restowed his cargo.

Will rubbed the towel through the canvas of his uniform. Prescott just stood still, his face the picture of tranquility, gripping his weapon gently. His mirrored lenses betrayed no sense of unease.

Harrison's voice rang out through everyone's earpieces. "Bravo team, in position."

"Alpha team on the move," Will spoke into his receiver. "Prescott."

The three men moved in unison, ten feet of spacing between them, down the street back toward the target building. Will felt his blood pump harder with each step, yet his hands seemed to become more steady. He aimed his rifle past Prescott and Mike at the target of their walk, the entrance to Mission. With each step his nerves quieted and his senses heightened. His eyes filtered out the chaos of the police lights. He knew his knuckles were no longer white. Fear was being replaced with something, else.

Prescott reached the front of the building and paused for Will and Mike to catch up. As soon as all three men were grouped, Prescott stepped forward again, moving to the far side of the entrance. His black shoes collided with a pile of red snow as he stepped quickly across the entrance.

"Alpha team, in position," Will whispered into his mic. "Breach on my count.

"Three.

"Two.

An explosion rocked the back alleyway. Screams echoed in Will's ear. A half second staccato of gunfire followed.

Prescott immediately pushed through the door before the cries ended. Mike and Will followed. The three men scanned the room in all directions, weapons raised, senses on alert.

No threat. No hostages.

Several overhead fixtures lit the room to a low, almost casual level. The bar was imposing. Wood and steel blended into thirty feet of bullet riddled concealment. The adjoining rooms to the right were a wreck. Tables were turned on their sides. Food and drinks were spilled over the floor. The smell of the various foods mixed with the lingering burn of freshly incinerated black powder. Plates, napkins, silverware and purses littered the floor.

Will quickly moved to the bar and leaned over, clear.

He kept his weapon trained on the large kitchen entrance near the end of the bar. Prescott and Mike moved to the back stairwell leading to the second floor. Frozen air pushed into the dining area from a fifteen foot hole ripped into the corner past the top of the stairs, rendering them impassable. A right boot lay on the ground. Charred bone protruded from the black leather hole and spurted blood on a white tablecloth laying tattered on the empty dance floor. A pink anklet with the words 'Speed Racer' revealed the owner as Flory.

Silence.

The quiet was almost as deafening as the gunfire and screams that dominated Will's ears only a moment before. Prescott reached the bottom stairs first, and glanced up into the stairwell's jagged gash. His left hand relinquished control of his rifle. The barrel tip slapped the hard tile floor with an audible metallic pop. He lifted from his athletic crouch to a rigid vertical stance. He reached up with his left hand and removed his glasses, dropping them to the floor as his hand found his hip. His mouth opened slightly, eyes wide.

A small, two inch in diameter shiny metal sphere dropped out from behind the wall above Prescott. It slammed into the floor, denting the tile but refused to bounce. Prescott began to raise his rifle.

He dropped to his knee, still looking up, rifle raising with his right arm as his left hand slammed into the floor and his torso hunched forward. Mike, in the adjoining dining room, lifted from the floor and sprung forward, toward the ball. Will felt a pull and stumbled forward. He caught himself with his left foot, stopping his forward momentum before being thrown backward by a large explosion. His back slammed into the wooden boards of the bar. A coat hook sliced his left eyebrow.

Prescott was engulfed in a white incendiary ball. He and Mike were shredded as a massive concussive force emanated from the sphere. Screams echoed through the cavernous barroom. A longhorn rattled from the wall and landed at Will's feet. Will regained his footing and aimed his rifle at the kitchen, then back to the stairwell. His ears were ringing and his head throbbed. His senses dulled and he rapidly blinked his eyes to clear his blurry vision.

Will could barely make out Sergeant Hess's voice in his ear, "Report. What the fuck is going on in there?" Will dazedly looked around. He felt liquid running down his face so he reached up to wipe away his sweat. His black fingerless gloves came away brownish in color, white fingers smeared with red blood. Will regained his composure and saw at his teammates' shattered bodies.

Will keyed his microphone to reply to Sergeant Hess. His heart leapt in his chest as he saw a shimmer round the corner of the stairwell moving at high velocity. Time froze for him. In the millisecond it took the object to cover the twenty five feet from the stairwell to the bar, his life flashed before his eyes.

Will saw fields of fiddler crabs playing on the soft sand of the Virginia beaches as they enjoyed low tide. He saw orange slices at soccer. He saw Meghan's goulden brown eyes sparkle, and Nancy's perfect lips. He saw graduation from parajump school.

His thoughts were interrupted as a rectangular blue color flashed in front of him. It seemed to arc around his body, and extended from the floor to just above his helmet, a mere inch away. As soon as the blue wall appeared, a small red mark defiled the pristine surface, directly in front of the bridge of his nose. The blue wall imploded upon the red mark into a small spinning ball and vanished. A bullet fell to the ground with a thud.

Will startled from his shock as a hand grabbed his collar and dragged him over the bar, slamming him against the bar rail. A hand went over his mouth and another pressed his rifle down so it pointed to the floor.

"I'm on your side. Relax," Will heard the man say in front of him. "I'm Vine. Do what I say if you want to live." The man removed his hand from Will's mouth, but maintained control over the gun. Will looked at him, and immediately knew he was not someone to fuck with. Will could see urgency, rage, and familiarity behind dark bloodstained eyes.

With a quick glance Will saw the man was solidly built at 5'9" and one hundred sixty five pounds. He had clean midnight black skin, and half centimeter length dark black curly hair. His face was slightly stubbly as though normally clean shaven, but hadn't had a chance to perform the grooming ritual in several days. A few flecks of stubble were a silver color, revealing his age.

"What the fuck is going on?" Will demanded.

"If you want to survive, if you want to get revenge, watch my back. Either you come with me or sit here and wait to die."

Will simply nodded in reply.

"Let's go," Vine stated. He readied his weapon and rounded the corner. He moved quickly to the kitchen entrance. "I need to clear the kitchen, get upstairs, and ensure our agent is safe. Then I'll fill you in."

Vine hugged the entrance's left edge as he nimbly stepped through the threshold and into the kitchen with his rifle at the ready. His rifle moved gracefully following his eyes, which occasionally darted rapidly while maintaining a purity of focus. He scanned the entire area in seconds. He moved along the left side of the room, peeking under the massive industrial exhaust fan. Will followed behind him only a fraction of a second later, weapon trained on the right side of the room as he moved to clear the other half of the area. There were too many places to hide.

Vine and Will converged on the rear server staircase. Vine took the lead and headed up the spiral station. The strike of Vine's heels on the metal steps rang out in the quiet kitchen. He moved quickly and Will hurried to keep up. Vine's rifle passed the top step and he emerged onto the second floor. He paused for a moment in surprise at the sight before him.

He blinked his eyes to regain focus, then continued up and stood firmly on the second floor as Will joined him. Everyone was seated for a meal, but no one was eating. No one was talking. To the right, a table with four plates had only three patrons seated. Their faces were white, life drained from their tear-stained faces. Spots of blood spattered their faces and clothing. The fourth chair was on its side, burned and broken to pieces, next to a young woman in a black cocktail dress curled limply on the floor.

At one table in the back left corner sat a man with his back to the landing. A large blood splash was on the wall to his left. His hands hung limp to his sides, head rolled back. His lunch partner was an older man with short wavy white hair. He murmured to himself in a seemingly endless, indecipherable stream of broken words. Blood was still smeared over the man's face where he had tried to clean himself with his napkin but failed. The babbling man was the only life in the sea of carnage.

"That's not my guy." Vine whispered to Will. "Stay here, watch my back."

As Vine approached, Will heard a stream of profanities escape his mouth. Vine tapped the mumbling man on the shoulder, who snapped out of his trance and emitted a quiet gasp of shock and fear. "It's okay," Vine said, slinging his rifle over his shoulder and grabbing the man by both shoulders.

"Relax. I'm one of the good guys. Tell me your name."

"Mar, Marcus," the man stammered. He cleared his throat. "I'm Marcus Shaw."

"Do I need to ask what the fuck happened, or do you just want to start talking?"

"He," Marcus paused, still not looking up. "He let me live. He," Marcus paused in confusion.

"Wha-" Gabe's voice ended with a soft gargle. Will pressed his earpiece.

"He said it doesn't matter what I do. That, that he's already, killed me, and my family." His voice broke with confusion.

Vine helped the senator to his feet. The older man stumbled and caught himself on Vine's shoulder. He steadied himself. "Why were you meeting with Wayne?" Vine asked.

"He's a work buddy. We go way back to Venezuela, before Maduro had us thrown out of the country. We've worked on a few projects since. He said he had to see me. He said this was the one I'd been waiting for. A result worthy of effort.

"Honestly, I thought he sounded crazy, but he's earned my trust. I never imagined this," Marcus' voice trailed off as he looked around the room. His gaze lingered over the body of his fallen friend. Marcus ran his red-stained hand through his hair and looked down at his feet in disbelief.

"Wayne was working with us," Vine interjected. "He was heading up a project of ours. I can't explain all the details to you now, but he was in a key position to unite the banks in an effort to work toward global prosperity. I can only assume he wanted political help from you in some way."

Marcus interrupted. "Whatever it is, I want to help. He had started explaining some of his plan for a specialized mutual f-"

A massive explosion from the street shattered the front entrance of the restaurant. Splintered wood and dust rained down upon the men and the building shook on its foundation. Several pipes began spewing water from the dislodged walls. All three men crouched down and covered their heads from the debris. Sgt. Hess and the entire force had been eliminated. No screams were heard, or needed.

"We need to get out of here," Vine laughed. He seemed to smile at chaos without escalating. He turned back toward the senator. "I'll come see you tomorrow at your home at eight in the evening. I'll explain more then. Welcome to the fight. Oh, don't mention us when you leave if you can." Vine glanced around quickly, then took off his small backpack and began to rummage through it.

After a few seconds he stopped searching through his pack and pulled out a small metallic case. He held the reflective chrome box in one hand and typed a numeric key code into the front. It popped open, revealing four circular bands three inches in diameter. Each band had a faint red light emanating from it as though made from a dying glow stick. Vine removed one of the bands and took a deep breath.

"Are you in? There's no going back after this."

Will nodded.

"Put this on your left wrist."

The band expanded to slide over Will's hand and tightened down when it reached his wrist. It wiggled, but didn't chafe. The red glow was present, but unobtrusive. Vine closed the case containing the three remaining bands and placed it back inside his backpack. He shouldered his pack, and let out a deep breath through his mouth. His shoulders sagged a full inch, a difference made more noticeable by the backpack peeking out behind his thick neck. He relaxed for the first time.

"Just a tip, when we get there, don't say anything about yourself. No name or date."

"No date?" Will asked in surprise. "Where are we going?"

"Just don't talk unless you have to," Vine stated, ignoring his question as he raised his left wrist. Will noticed a similar but larger red glowing band on Vine's wrist. The thin band was attached to a much larger wrist panel with a small computer screen attached. He keyed in something into the screen and paused. Will's band changed from a red color to a light amber, and finally to green. Vine's band remained reddish a moment longer, then turned green. The screen attached to the band clearly stated "Kuruka" above a small green circle.

"You'll understand in a second. Whether you like it or not, you're in." Vine stated, and pushed the green circle.

Chapter 2

Will lurched forward, falling to his knees, and vomited. He looked up to be sure his eyes hadn't tricked him, then recoiled and heaved again. Through his retching he heard Vine's laughter. He groaned and and leaned back, still on his knees, and wiped his mouth with his sleeve.

Will looked around. Somehow the back alleyway outside of Mission became the inside of a large busy warehouse. Vine pressed the button on his wristband, and in that instant the room flashed, and Will's stomach leapt into his throat. Will groaned as he saw a man approach.

The man appeared two inches shorter than Will, and a bit overweight. His white hair was slicked back and pushed to the left so his left ear was covered. The left side of his face was heavily scarred with fiery red blotches. While a bushy white beard covered the man's face, Will could barely make out the same fiery red blotches of scars under the beard. His left arm and leg bore the same scarring as the left side of his face.

The right side of his face had only one blemish, a straight line scar was distinctly visible between his right temple and the middle of his nose, disappearing under a black eyepatch. He dressed very casually in a white short sleeve silk shirt, black shorts, and red thong sandals.

The man ascended the two steps from the floor of the warehouse to the platform where Will and Vine stood, looked at Will, then to Vine.

"Who's this, a pet?" the bearded man asked Vine while signaling someone behind him to come over. His voice was stern, matching his composure. His shoulders were held back and the stare from his left eye inspired only compliance.

"A new recruit," Vine replied, as he helped Will to his feet. Looking around, Will saw the warehouse was not what he originally thought. First, he realized he was standing on an elevated stage. Then he noticed it was actually a rather complex looking operation similar to the old operations centers at some of the major bases he'd operated out of in Iraq, only larger.

The room stretched at least one hundred meters long and fifty wide. The cavernous facility appeared sterile with industrial grey paint on the walls. While three of the walls were almost entirely plain, the wall to the left side of the platform was adorned with four rows of evenly spaced green tree emblems, each one foot squared. The trees resembled silhouettes of redwoods from the Muir Woods of California. The top three rows stretched the entire length of the wall. The fourth and bottom row was centered and only had seven of the emblems. With the room being at least fifty feet high, there was plenty of space above and below the redwoods for more rows to be added.

Taking in the activity of the room, Will noticed at least two hundred men and women working intently at tables scattered about the room. Will's scan of the room was interrupted as a woman in white carrying a small white stick in her right hand appeared behind the scarred man on the steps. The woman approached Vine, held the device in front of his left eye for a moment, then his right.

As she inspected Vine, Will watched. She stood at 5'8" in tight white pants and a white dress shirt, smartly tucked into her pants. A black belt offered stark contrast to the white of her clothing. She had her raven black hair in a short pixie cut and ruby red lips. She had a slender build, but looked fit. Her face was firm but soft. Her eyes and the corners of her lips were marked with several small wrinkles.

"You're good," she reported to Vine.

She moved to Will and held up the device in front of his face. Will recoiled and grabbed her hand. It felt soft and warm in his grasp. He looked into her eyes and saw vibrant blue irises staring at him warmly. They radiated a kindness and grace he'd never seen before. He blinked a moment, then noted that while her eyes were crystal clear they were surrounded by a thin ring revealing she was wearing contact lenses.

"Relax, we're just checking your vitals. We need to make sure you aren't bringing anything nasty with you. This is just a simple medical scan to see what pathogens you might have. We can't have your ignorance starting an epidemic," she said. Will let go of her hand and stood upright, still feeling a little queasy. She moved the device in front of his right eye and Will saw a quick purple flash of light. She repeated the process again with his left eye.

"He's good." She reported to the bearded man, and

quickly turned and walked back down the steps. As she stepped down Will noted that she moved with grace despite wearing shoes with a several inch heel.

“Both of you, come with me for a debriefing," the bearded man said and turned toward a group at a nearby workstation. “Get someone to clean up this mess." He indicated the vomit-covered concrete platform where Will stood, then walked away. “Fucking rookies,” Will swore he heard grumbled from the white beard.

Vine shrugged towards the door and followed after the white haired man. Will spit onto the ground, wiped his mouth, and followed. He stepped down the two steps to the main floor area and headed across the room. Few people even glanced in his direction for more than a moment.

He kept walking after Vine and looked back at the raised platform where he just left. It appeared entirely normal. It was simply a square concrete stage elevated about a foot off the main floor. Aside from his influence, the platform was otherwise unblemished. Will turned and continued walking after Vine, glancing around at the people in the room. While they were all uniform in their focus on their current task, their dress and appearance could not have been more different.

Will glanced at four people working at a table near the door where he was heading. The first man was in standard black dress pants and purple dress shirt. His black dress shoes were brightly polished and matched his thin black belt. He was working with a strikingly dressed woman.

Her short brown hair flowed from underneath a dark brown poofy hat with firm black military style brim. She also had a clear visor over her left eye, disappearing around the side of her head and connecting to her ear. Lowering his eyes, Will noticed she was wearing a long sleeve white shirt with large puffy shoulders, disappearing under a tan waist cincher. The corset had suspenders rising from the top front sides and around the back of her neck. Below the corset was a thick dark brown belt matching her hat, affixed to royal purple pants. The pants ended in sturdy looking brown boots with large raised platform soles.

Across the table from them Will observed their two companions. Another woman sat, wearing a light pink sundress with pearls. Her strawberry blonde hair fell playfully to the top of her slender neck and was neatly contained under a thin white headband. Her athletic pale white legs extended from beneath the pink dress and ended in conservative black flats. The man sitting to her right shone. He wore a bright silver vest with neon green shoulder pads and stripes down the sides of his ribs, ending in silver and neon green pants.

Will walked past them quickly, noticing that the other tables' workers were equally outlandishly dressed. They never glanced in his direction, focused on whatever was being discussed at the workstation. Will walked through the back doorway behind Vine and the bearded man.

He stepped into a long somber gray corridor, at least one hundred feet long with doors scattered on each side and a door at the end. The air smelled stale and confined, almost recycled. As the door closed to the warehouse, the low bustle of the workers was muted, leaving Will only the sound of the footsteps and breathing of the two men in front of him. They headed into the nearest door on the right. Will followed and entered a small conference room.

The door closed behind the men with a soft hiss of air being sealed inside. The newest room was equally bland and stale. The air felt thicker here with even poorer ventilation. The walls were the same industrial gray. A solid gray rectangular table dominated the room with six white rolling chairs surrounding it. The floor matched the mechanical color of the walls.

"Take a seat and we'll get you up to speed," the bearded man stated. "Vine, do we need him for debriefing your mission, or does he just need standard indoc?"

"No, he didn't get involved until the last second. Have him checked out by the staff and get him brought up to speed. You and I need to talk about the next step. I think it's fucked," Vine replied with a smile and a shake of his head.

"I can tell. Okay, go get Alum and Grom. Tell them to come in here to check him out and bring him up to speed."

"Yes sir," Vine replied, then looked at Will. "Hand me your wristband."

Will grabbed the still green band from his left wrist. He slid it over his hand and noticed it return to an amber color. He handed it to Vine who quickly removed his pack and returned the band to its proper case, re-shouldered his pack, and walked out the door.

"Okay, let me get you the basics before everyone gets here. I'm sure you have a lot of questions. Grom will take care of that," the bearded man stated. "I'm Dr. G. I'm in charge of this little operation here. Everything that goes on here goes through me first. We're in the middle of our current campaign, and we'll try to find a way to make you useful."

"Where are we?" Will asked.

"I can't tell you that until you're checked out," Dr. G. replied. "For now, just realize you're green, but if you're able to think adaptively, you'll catch on. If not, the wa" He stopped mid sentence as the woman in white walked into the room.

Dr. G. stood. "New guy, this is Alum. She'll check you out to make sure you're okay. Apparently you're already a burden. Grom will be taken away from his usual duties to cater to you. There is only one thing you need to know. Forget your old life.

"Don't tell anyone your name or anything about your past. Tonight you'll need to have a new name, a call sign to go by while you're with us, unless you have one in mind already. We can't just keep calling you new guy forever. Let me be clear. You violate this, I will personally hurt you."

Will glanced up, smirking at the familiarity of the safety briefing. However, when his eyes locked with Dr. G. his smirk faded. He cleared his throat, "A call sign?" Will asked. "Why?"

"It's for your own protection and that of your family. You'll understand soon. Just think of something you want to go by from now on. Try to keep it simple. Oh, and welcome to the fight," Dr. G. added as he walked out the door.

Every move he made seemed concise, determined not to waste an ounce of energy or time. Even his arm sway was perfectly in-line, not crossing his body with wasted effort. His left eye focused exactly where he walked. Alum turned her head to watch him leave, then looked back to Will. She had a deceptive smile on her face as though she was trying to remain stoic but failed.

"Well, that's no way to make a proper introduction. I'm Alum," she said, holding out her right hand. Will shook her hand, noting her gentle handshake. "Don't worry, I know you're a little confused and can't exactly hold up your end of the introduction yet. Later you can try again. And don't worry about him, he's an acquired taste." She smiled gently as she placed a small medical kit on the table between herself and Will.

"So, are you some kind of nurse?" Will asked.

"I'm a doctor," she corrected curtly. "I'm sure you've had quite a traumatic day. Recruitment day is always a bit off-putting. Take off your shirt." She opened her case and took out a black rectangle that looked like a ruler. She hesitated and the edges of her lips trembled upwards momentarily. "I remember when I was first recruited. It's always a shock when you first run into the NPs. You seem like the composed type so I'm sure you'll be fine, but if you do have any trouble sleeping or anything just let me know and I'll see what I can do to help."

"NPs?" Will replied, tossing his shirt onto the table along with his other gear.

"New Puritans," she answered. She reached out and placed the ruler device vertically on Will in the middle of his chest down to his belly button. It immediately beeped, and Will felt it suck to his chest. "Imagine someone with the conviction of righteousness, a spartan upbringing, and zero morality. They kill without hesitation and without remorse. God's will and all that." She closed her eyes as her voice trembled. She paused and took a deep breath.

"Well, you can imagine we've all had similar experiences to you. A former agent of ours named Rana saved me, but it was too late for my friends. I was just an engineer and had never seen that kind of violence before. I was in pretty bad shape when I arrived. Everyone here helped me recover, and I've been here ever since.

"You'll find we have a very good community. After my first few years I started helping out with our campaign. I'm sure Dr. G. will find a use for you. He's very good at finding people's strengths." She pulled a small transparent plastic square out of her case and studied it intently. A jumble of words and lines scrolled across the face of the device.

As she glanced down at the square, a man walked into the room. He was short and frail. A white dress shirt with long sleeves popped out from under a dark navy blue vest. His forearms looked lost of an ocean of space as they popped out from the relatively cavernous arm holes. Ten gold buttons lined the front of the vest from belt to sternum. A thin black tie reached from the white collar to the top of the dark vest.

From the blue vest downward the man was wearing maroon pants tied off to calf high black boots. Four gold buckles locked each of them to his legs. His upper face was covered in large clear glasses like a fighter pilot helmet minus the helmet. Thick spiked brown hair popped at least five inches above his head, making his total height closer to 5'11". Will guessed the guy couldn't be older than sixteen.

"All of your vitals are within normal ranges. Your heart rate is elevated and you show signs of high stress. Fairly normal given what's happened to you today. Based on the scan, you don't have any pathogens we need to be afraid of. I'll scan you on a regular routine if you go on any missions. We never know what new biological threats we may encounter in the field." She reached into her case and produced a vial of small white pills. “Take one tonight before bed to help you sleep. Otherwise, I think you’re fully operational. Try not to get too overwhelmed. This is the start of a crazy day for you."

“Start?”

Alum ignored him and turned to the new arrival. “I’m done here. Where’s Grom?"

“Vine couldn’t find him, so he sent me over."

“He’s all yours. Don’t have too much fun in the armory," she chided. She grabbed her case, took one last lingering glance at Will, and left.

The man reached out his hand and firmly shook Will’s. His grip seemed strong for his size. Will guessed he was overcompensating. When he spoke, the boy’s voice matched his bone density. It wavered and did injustice to his South African accent.

“I’m Griz. I’m the tech officer here and a field operative. Apparently they want me to get you mission-ready ASAP," he said, standing next to the table. “That means I have to give you a crash course on weaponry and other technologies we utilize in the field. I have no idea why they’re voiding normal protocols for you.” Griz paused as a frown came over his face. His eyes moistened almost imperceptibly. “Let’s start by getting a quick biometric scan from you to give you access."

“Can you start by explaining what’s going on around here?" Will asked as he pulled his undershirt back on.

“Sure. First thing is, I don’t exactly know when or where we are. No one does aside from Dr. G," Griz stated while reaching into his pocket. “We are known simply as ‘The Bulwark’. Depending on which timeline you’re from, mankind either had an extinction level event, or near so. Our job is to change that. This is my second campaign as part of The Bulwark. My understanding is that Dr. G. is currently leading this as his third campaign. No one knows what was before him."

"Wait, what timeline I'm from?"

"Yea, no one told you yet?"

"Told me what? I just got here."

"We jump to different times and try to alter the future to prevent humanity from killing itself. That's our mission at least. How'd you get recruited anyway?" he asked, holding up a small cylinder.

Will paused and looked down at his feet, then back to Griz. "My monday morning got fucked."

Griz hesitated, then popped open the cylinder to reveal a glass panel on the inside. "Right. Place your right thumb on the screen," he stated flatly while waiting for Will to comply. "Well, don't feel bad. Everyone has a similar story here. We all were potential collateral damage for an NP mission and someone here saved us.

"My family was on vacation in our time. Mal blew up the entire hotel we were staying at to stop a United Nations gathering that was setting up new environmental sanctions. As Mal was making his getaway, he killed everyone in his path, including my parents.

"My sister and I were just kids. My parents weren't even targets. We were just standing in the wrong place at the wrong time. He had just killed my parents and was about to execute us when Dr. G. showed up. If Dr. G. had shown up half a second later we would have died. Now we're here. We're the lucky ones.

"This will sting a little." Griz said as he closed the cylinder around Will's finger. Will winced and recoiled. "Reading complete. Uploading your biometrics, now." Griz paused, his eyes squinted and he cocked his head to the right. "That's strange, it's giving me an error trying to create a new entry."

"Why would anyone blow up a UN building that was setting up environmental sanctions?"

Green text popped up in a small font on Griz's visor. He paused a moment, and tapped the side of the lense causing the text to disappear from the screen.

"Look, we have to get moving with your tech indoc. Vine wants you on mission tomorrow morning. Apparently you're his new partner." Griz frowned and furrowed his eyebrows. "He can tell you the rest." His frail voice broke. "I'll figure out your biometrics later. I should have everything I need.

"First, what do you want to be called? Make it something unrecognizable from your former life. The NPs take special pride in eliminating Bulwark members from history. If you die fighting, we might be able to save you. If they ever catch you, they'll get your true identity. If they do, they go to your time, and if they can, they kill you and sometimes your entire family line. That way, there's no way we can ever save you.

"If the NPs take you alive, there's nothing we can do. That's why it's also key to follow the rules here and never let anyone know your true time and name of origin. NPs try to get as much information as possible from captured Bulwark members, and they'll kill entire extended families with the hopes of eliminating even one Bulwark operative from the fight. They have no limits."

"Call me Nac," Will stated flatly.

"Why Knack?"

"I like how it sounds," Nac replied.

"Okay, Nac, whatever. Let's get you weapon-ready for tomorrow's mission. I'll try to explain more about our mission as we go. We have an armory down the hallway. Follow me." Griz paused for Nac to stand, then walked out the door with Nac following closely. They turned right out of the door and walked down the insipid hallway. "A lot of the weapons you'll see here are simple adaptations of the same weapons throughout time. Just try not to be blown away by new tech. After all, a rifle just replaces a bow and arrow's tension with gas pressure for method of projectile and quiver with a magazine for storage. These upgrades are similar.

"My understanding is your mission with Vine tomorrow morning is to go back to your time and secure a recent recruit as a forward asset," Griz stated.

"What does that mean?"

"Vine must have someone we think can be useful in our current campaign. I'm guessing you'll make contact with him, walk him through our current plan of action, and try to convince him to join us. What's really surprising is Vine taking you under his wing. He's been a solo operator for as long as I can remember," Griz stated with an agitated tone. "They always said he gets special permission to operate alone. I think Dr. G. has a soft spot for him. It's not fair."

Griz stopped at the last door on the left and quickly opened it, beckoning for Nac to go ahead. Nac was met with another corridor, only this one was lined with weapons from throughout time. Starting to his left was an ancient and heavily worn looking bow and arrow. Across the hall, in another display, a large stone was lashed with leather strips to an inch thick and foot long wooden stick.

As Nac walked down the long hallway, he saw the bows improve in quality until becoming crossbows, flintlocks, and rifles. To his right shoulder the stone hammer was the first in a line of progressively sharper swords, axes, and bayonets. Halfway down the row it became armors of various types, leather greaves and chainmail all the way to kevlar body armor. At the end of the line was a thin black belt with a three inch square black box attached.

Nac opened the door at the end of the hallway with a gentle hiss of escaping air. Griz cocked his head in surprise. "I guess it uploaded your biometrics to the database after all," he stated, beckoning Nac inside.

Looking around the new room, Nac immediately smiled. Weapons of all shapes and sizes adorned the walls all around him. It was a dream come true. To his right he saw massive artillery units ranging from long range ballistics to handheld rocket launchers. To his left, a thirty foot wall was adorned with rifles of every combination. Some had scopes and laser sights while others had attached grenade launchers.

"Fuck yes," he said, grinning ear to ear. The entrance to the room was a large open space leading to a row of booths, at least ten in all. The booths looked out over the firing range. The range had an entirely empty target area and an earthen backdrop. A large command console sat in the front corner of the room overlooking the firing booths.

"We don't have enough time to go through all of the weapons, but I'm going to give you quick training on some basic models. Over time you can familiarize yourself with the rest of the weapons." Griz walked toward the wall to the right. "Let's start with armor, as this is pretty basic stuff." He reached out and grabbed a vest. His voice became more resolute as he described each item.

“This is the standard light infantry vest. It will stop most small arms non-specialized rounds from penetration. It’s ideal for most missions you go on, but NPs typically have specialized weapons, charged or explosive rounds. It’s lightweight at around three pounds. You get hit with a normal round, it’ll hurt like hell, but won’t kill you." Griz knocked on the front of the vest with his hand making a dull thud sound.

“Next up is a shield. This isn’t your standard knight of the round table or Spartan shield. This is the modern version.” Griz smiled, holding up a black belt with a three inch solid black box attached.

“That was the last in the row of armor in the hallway outside?" Nac asked.

“Correct. It’s the most advanced personal shield we have. It forms a barrier in all directions around you. Any round strikes it, and it will absorb the impact, no matter where it is. Someone shoots you in the knees, this’ll take it. It absorbs up to five thousand joules of force. It’ll stop anything from a concussion grenade to a sniper round. Remember, it only holds one charge, so if you see this thing go off, move out of the way or the second round will kill you.”

Griz tapped the black buckle. “Inside this compartment is a capacitor to store the shield charge and a set of kinetic gears that generate a charge as you move. Depending on your movement, it can recharge as quickly as five minutes. The shield deploys based on detecting high velocity incoming objects. Therefore, it won’t discharge for knives, fists, or anything moving at relatively slow speeds. If deployed, it will create a blue wall around the incoming object and stop it in its tracks. The buckle easily attaches and reattaches to any object."

"I think I've seen it in action already."

"Good, let's move on to weaponry." Griz patted Nac on the shoulder and walked across the room to the wall full of knives. His command of the room seemed complete as he reached down and lifted a four inch steel knife with centimeter black steel guards and leather finger grooves ringing the handle. "Here are your basic assault knives. See the labeling? Some are for throwing, some for hand to hand combat. Some have discharges. Familiarise yourself with them later and choose the one you like best.

"Next we have pistols. There are two basic models that we utilize here, but you can customize your weapon any way you want. Grom, our armory tech, will be here soon to get you fully customized. I suggest playing with both and seeing which basic weapon has the best feel. As usual, weapons can have customized ammo, explosive and electric rounds. Explosive are great for unarmored targets, while electric can kill an armored target regardless of where it hits as long as their shield is down. Shoot someone in their foot, and the electric charge immediately triggers and gives them an unpleasant end," Griz said.

"Then there's the customizable rifle, the M-10." Griz took a small rifle down from the wall. "Its basic configuration has three fire options, semi-automatic, automatic, and burst. The stock makes it almost one hundred percent recoilless for accuracy even when fully unleashed. Where it gets fun are the underbarrel configurations. Some go with the grenade launcher, others choose shotgun attachments. Choose for yourself.

"As you can see there are plenty of other caliber options. Choose the best weapon for the mission, but the

M-10 is the most customizable. Similar to the pistols, rounds can be customized for either electric or explosive. Personally, I think it's a bit on the small side. I like to pack a bigger punch." His voice trembled with the final statement.

Griz placed the rifle back on the wall rack and grabbed a shiny silver orb from a nearby pedestal.

"I've seen that before," Nac glumly commented, taking a deep breath.

"That's a grenade. It has three settings. First is your basic smoke grenade for concealment. The second setting is my favorite, the void grenade. It's your standard concussion grenade with an added element of creating a vacuum before explosion. Basically, it pulls your target closer to the explosion for increased effect. For the final setting, the grenade can be set for flash to incapacitate the target without killing it. All three settings are here on this selector. Press the setting you need and throw."

Nac heard a booming voice behind him. "Don't forget to show him the drone feature, Griz. For a technical officer, you don't seem to fully understand the technology."

A hulk of a man stood near the entrance. The man wore black boots and dark blue and black camouflage pants. He also wore a black shirt with a green tree, matching the emblems on the wall from the arrival point, emblazoned on the left chest. Below a thick dark brown mustache he was chewing on a weathered, unlit cigar. His eyes were barely visible under a matching camouflage boonie hat. His biceps strained at the fabric of his shirt, ending in large veiny forearms.

"I'm Grom, the armorer around here. Griz, why don't you go fuck off somewhere while I get the new meat spun up on the real weapons here instead of just the crap you fancy. If you listen to him, you'll go into battle with more weight on your back than a Nepali sherpa," Grom boomed while scowling at Griz. "I'll get him fully equipped."

Nac laughed as he noticed Griz turn away and exit back to the hallway without a discussion, his pale face burning crimson red.

"Kid thinks he's going to be a fucking futuristic Teddy Roosevelt, riding into battle on a fucking bear while shooting electric rounds at mechanical demons," Grom laughed and extended his hand. "He's a good kid though."

Nac reached out to shake his hand. "I'm Nac. Anyone ever tell you you're a dead ringer for Sergeant Slaughter?"

"Who?"

"Nevermind, I'm already breaking the rules by saying that. So, what kind of good shit did Griz neglect to show me?"

"We've got a few hours until dinner. I think that gives me time to walk you through some of the rifle section," Grom stated and slapped Nac on the back with his colossal forearms. "They told me you know your way around weapons. You're going to love some of this technology, especially the firing range."

Chapter 3

The next morning:

Nac bolted upright. His breath came quickly through his open mouth. Sweat poured down his forehead. His bed sheets were soaked with sweat. He closed his eyes and breathed deeply through his nose, slowly clenching and unclenching his fists. He glanced at the nearby clock and realized he only had ten minutes until he needed to be up. He slipped his legs from under the blanket, placing them firmly on the cold sterile floor. He rubbed his face with both hands to wipe the sleep from his eyes.

He stood and dropped to the ground. He moved through his customary series of sun salutations to start his day. Right lunge to left lunge, up dog and down dog combined to wake his body up and steady his mind for the chaotic day ahead. With each movement his mind shifted from the tumultuous thoughts and demands to focus only on his breath. He regained his footing, breathing heavily, and looked around his new world.

A small white metal double bed was tucked neatly into the corner. A matching white foot squared board jutted out of the side of the bed to serve as a nightstand. Nac's red Nationals baseball rally towel sat atop nightstand with the alarm serving as a paperweight. The rest of the room was entirely bare aside from a small closet near the entryway. The room was no larger than a ten by ten foot cube. He leaned down and quickly made his bed, gray woolen military grade comforter on top of thin white cotton sheets. The red rally towel was the only color in the otherwise drab room.

Nac walked over and opened his small closet. Four simple camouflage uniforms hung neatly in order, all facing to the right. On the left were hanging drawers of undergarments. Socks, boxers, and black t-shirts were folded neatly in their respective bins. He reached into the closet and grabbed a black undershirt. The snug fit warmed him from the chill morning air. He quickly put on the camouflage pants and all-black combat boots and black socks. He pulled them over his feet and stood. He frowned as the horrors of the previous day returned. He grabbed the sink to steady himself.

Nac dropped his head and closed his eyes. His knuckles turned white as his grip tightened. He breathed deeply. He looked up, then back down again, as the memories of four tours of duty flooded his brain.

Nac snapped out of his trance as he heard a strong knock at the door a few feet to his right. He walked over and opened the unblemished white door, noting a screen display on the wall showing Vine standing in the hallway. Outside, Vine waited dressed in his matching camouflage pants and black crew neck shirt. The same redwood tree was emblazoned on both of their chests over their hearts. As Nac opened the door, Vine grinned, then asked, "Ready for your first day of school?"

Nac nodded with a sleep strained smile, and walked out into the dormitory hallway. The hall was equally bland, unblemished white doors spaced every few meters were the only blot on the otherwise smooth grey walls. They walked through the small maze of the dormitory wing in silence. After a quick stop in the armory with Grom to get geared up, they went to the main operations center where Nac initially arrived.

Vine paused as he neared the entrance and reached his hand towards the floor. An orange and blonde tabby cat, at least fifteen pounds in all, jumped onto his arm and struggled to climb to his shoulders. It finally settled in, a claw clinging to his ear. It rubbed its head against Vine's face.

"Hey Benz," he whispered, and tossed a cracker onto the floor. The cat stared at Vine in disbelief, then rose, and carefully climbed down his body, talons fully bared for safety. It jumped to floor, grabbed the cracker, and slowly scampered around the corner.

Once inside, the two men headed to a control center on the left side of the room. Dr. G. was already there. He stood in his same red thong sandals, white short sleeve button up shirt, and black shorts. He was intense in his movements and concise with his words as he spoke with Griz and another woman whom Nac had spotted when he first arrived. Her short reddish blonde hair flowed just past her neck, resting on a white blouse with dark polka dots. A green belt cut into the middle of her blouse, which puffed out from under the belt covering the top of a conservative green pencil skirt.

Griz, on the other hand, looked even more outlandish than before. His thick spiked brown hair still stood at least five inches tall above his visor-covered smooth face. Otherwise, he could've passed for a Civil War general. He wore a dark navy blue unbuttoned overcoat with at least twenty shiny golden buttons running along the chest. His shoulders were adorned with golden tassels. Underneath was a matching navy blue vest with ten matching buttons. The heavy garment created the vision of his shoulders being nearly twice the size of his waist.

His wrists looked like straws, barely filling the sleeve. A white buttoned collar was barely visible above the vest. A large black belt with massive golden buckle cleaved the blue vest. Below were matching navy blue pants resting on shiny hand polished black dress shoes. "General Babyface," Nac thought.

Hearing the men approach, the group turned toward the newcomers. "Nac, this is our operations chief, Diana. Diana, all yours," Dr. G. stated.

"Thank you, sir. We've come up with a plan to move forward with our current campaign given the events that happened on your last mission, Vine. Nac, what do you know of the current campaign?"

"I spent all day getting processed and having fun in the armory. Grom filled me in on some of the background, I think, but no one told me what we're up to today."

"Too long didn't read? Okay, let's just do a quick recap to be safe, then be on our way. Our current plan is to blend natural human desire for affluence with our goal of creating a future where humans can effectively survive. Wayne was our contact with Goldman Sachs. Dr. G. recruited him. He was the agent Vine was attempting to reach yesterday at Mission. While his loss is a blow to our fight, we think this is our best play.

"Wayne was running lead on uniting several of the

top banks in the world to create a specialized mutual fund. The point is to create an investable fund that would automatically divert ten percent of all investment funds into this new fund, we call the human fund.

"The human fund's performance will be tied to global prosperity, specifically poverty levels, access to clean water, food, shelter, education, and levels of pollution. There will also be an automatic increase or decrease based on peace. Our hope is this fund will tie wealth to helping others, creating an incentive for preserving the Earth."

"In short, motivate people to improve the world and humanity's future through harnessing their own greed," Dr. G. interrupted.

Diana paused, brushing a small strand of hair from her face revealing her soft brown eyes. She glanced toward Nac quickly. He noticed her eyes were ringed with gold. "We're going to have Senator Marcus Shaw take his place. As a prior CEO of Bank of America and with his current political office, he's an even better candidate to lead the efforts. Your mission today is to recruit the senator to join our fight. If successful, well, hopefully we can save the world. If not, it's back to zero. If he joins us, we'll assign him protection to ensure his safety. Given the NP activity on this one, it's safe to say we're on the right track."

"The right track? What do you mean?" Nac asked.

"If this mission were futile, The NPs wouldn't try to stop us. They don't care if we waste our time. Their only desire is to ensure the end comes." Dr. G curtly answered. "If you want to take off the training wheels, you need to shift your thinking. The NPs can jump also. All of our campaigns, we're effectively just stationary defenses. Targets. We take what gains we get."

"Right, now we can't exactly have you all heading into this mission in full combat regalia," Diana added. "Griz will show you to the tailor before your jump and ensure you blend in. Remember, you're going to be meeting with a member of U.S. Congress in 2015. It's important to look the part. The congressman is currently staying in a condo in Southeast Washington D.C. near the Nationals Baseball stadium." She pressed a button on the large vertical plastic screen which seamlessly changed to display a map of Washington, D.C. in 2015. She tapped again and it smoothly zoomed into Southeast D.C.

"His family is back home in South Carolina so you shouldn't have any distractions. We'll set you up to jump into 5 March 2015 at eighteen hundred hours on a walking trail on the northwest side of the Anacostia River in waterfront park." She indicated a spot two to three miles east of the baseball stadium. "You'll have to go on foot to the senator's house here. It's a few miles walk, and there are lots of federal buildings in between so make sure you don't try to cut through any guarded areas. The goal of this mission is to remain undetected. Vine, you hear me?"

"I got it," Vine replied. "I learned my lesson in Denver," he added with a smile.

"Good. Total mission duration should be under five hours for you. Griz, they're all yours."

"Right, follow me and we'll get you outfitted." He led them over to a large black device slightly bigger than a phone booth standing in the corner. "Nac, if you step into the machine I'll load up a basic configuration for you. Step inside and confirm the selection on the screen."

Nac stepped into the machine and closed the door. Inside was a small screen with the clothing selection displayed and an empty rack for hanging clothes. He changed the color of the sweater from bright red to a dark green and hit confirm. The booth hummed, and Nac felt his entire body vibrate gently. His clothes melted away, and were replaced by the clothes displayed on the screen.

Soft blue jeans materialized on his legs. His feet lowered to the floor as boots were replaced with brown shoes. A tight white undershirt appeared followed by a thick cashmere V-neck sweater. A large brown bomber jacket with exposed soft white fleece lined interior, belt, and thick red scarf appeared on the rack along with a spiral tie dye knit stocking cap. Grabbing the extra clothing from the rack, Nac stepped outside. When the fleece touched his skin, its fluffiness served as a demonstration to the progress of humanity.

“That was incredible. How long do these clothes last?

“As long as you keep them up. They’re just like any other," Griz stated. “This is a tailor from the 23rd century. Most people call it a polybox. It breaks down your old clothes into pellets for re-use. It can be configured to create anything you want. There’s one in the dormitory area so you can create clothes of your choice since I’m guessing you didn’t bring much with you."

As Griz talked, Vine stepped into the booth. “Why polybox?” Nac asked glancing to Vine popping out of the polybox wearing a yellow sweater with a black overcoat.

“The inventor initially only made it to work with one specific chemical composition of polyester fabrics. It’s evolved over time.” Griz answered and handed Nac a small backpack. “This is for any additional gear you want to take with you. Inside you’ll find your jump drive. It’s the wrist band all of our field agents wear. It is essential for jump safety."

Nac reached into his pack and removed a tray matching the one Vine used the previous day. He opened it and removed a thick armband about two inches thick. He slid it over his wrist and felt its adhesive base grip his forearm. He watched as the screen readout immediately turned on with the world, "calibrating". The end of the band closest to his hand matched the small band from the day before and glowed a soft amber color.

"Once done calibrating, it'll tune into your life force. If anything happens that would or does kill you, it transports you immediately back to us. That way NPs can't ever search a downed agent and gain intelligence," Griz stated.

"How?"

"It senses all of your vitals; stress, blood pressure, pulse etc. For instance, if your pulse stops, you immediately teleport back to us so we can hopefully revive you. On any mission we send you on, we wait at the launch point for your return with our medical officer at the ready. All missions return here exactly thirty seconds after departure. In the event of a forced evacuation by the band, you'll arrive sixty seconds after departure. Also, once you jump, the band can't be removed by force. Any attempt to remove the band will trigger a return jump."

Nac placed his remaining gear and armaments into his backpack and hefted it over his back. "I think I'm ready."

Vine nodded, heading toward the launch point where Nac had arrived only the day before. Alum stood nearby with her medical kit ready.

Nac and Vine stepped up onto the platform, backpacks shouldered. Griz walked over to a large command console resting at the base of the launch point and keyed the screen.

"Ready?" he asked.

Both men nodded in return.

"Clench your stomach," Vine whispered to Nac.

Nac glanced away from Griz's countdown to look quizzically at Vine. He felt his stomach lurch as the room disappeared. In an instant the warmth of the command center was replaced by the brutal cold of Washington, D.C. winter. Nac dropped to his knees. He coughed for a moment and vomited into the white snow.

Vine chuckled and helped Nac to his feet. "You'll get the hang of it eventually. I lost it my first few jumps too. Just pretend someone's about to punch you in the stomach. It works for me. Or, you can always appear white girl wasted."

"Thanks for the tip," Nac replied.

"I can help demonstrate next time, if you want."

"An offer only a true gentleman would make, but no thanks."

Vine tapped his wristband and smiled. "Let me know if you change your mind. You'll need to familiarize yourself with all of the tools on the time drive. It immediately adapts to a time readout of current local time. It also has advanced maps to display the terrain given our time, and of course, a compass." He glanced down at his band for a moment and turned to get a proper westward bearing. "Now, before we go, know that Mal and other NP agents are masters of the ambush. Keep your guard up. If you feel like anything is off, speak up. Hopefully this mission will be a walk in the park."

The two men hefted their small backpacks and began trudging down the waterfront trail to the Southwest with the Anacostia River to their left. The frigid water was empty and unused. The shoreline was separated from the water by several feet of refuse jostling in the water as tiny waves lapped against the land. Both men pulled their coats tight over their bodies and ensured the buttons were fully done up, protection against the biting cold of winters in the district. Vine covered his face with the tail end of his scarf.

They walked through the open navy yard waterfront walkway. To their left they saw several old Navy warships in retirement, now mere tourist attractions. To the right was a ten foot high ominous black metal fence with spiked posts every six inches, protecting an obviously secure area inside.

The men continued down the pathway toward the baseball stadium. The massive structure made even the nearby high rise condominiums look small. Nac remembered making that very walk with his old girlfriend Charlotte only a year prior. She'd left him after two years because she stopped being fun, or because of his drinking, he wasn't sure. Nac reached down to his pants pocket, realising he had left his towel back in his room at the Bulwark compound. A sense of unease clenched his stomach.

The men continued to walk toward the stadium and turned to the right. Nac checked the GPS feature on his device and noted the small white indicator marking his presence steadily moving closer to the blue destination indicator of the Senator's home. They quickly reached the front of a large new looking tan building. The plainness of the tan building was offset by a shiny metallic awning with a bright orange word "Velocity" emblazoned on the front.

Nac and Vine opened the door to the main entryway

and stepped inside. Vine held his wristband up to the key fob reader and the door unlocked. “For most older technologies the band will give instant access to any electronic entry points, even those with biometric security." The two men walked to the elevators. They unbuttoned their coats and removed their scarves as the climate controlled lobby soothed the aches from the cold outside.

Vine checked his band readout as they stepped inside the small elevator. “I hope you aren’t superstitious.” He pressed the button for the thirteenth floor. The door began to close, only to be interrupted by a hand shooting through the opening. Three large men stepped inside.

Standing side by side, they separated Nac and Vine in the back of the small elevator. Nac felt his blood begin to pump faster. His heart raced and his fingers rubbed against his palms. His eyes darted from one man to the next. He was startled as the elevator began to rise with a jolt, causing him to raise his hands in a defensive position. One of the men roughly bumped Nac as he removed his jacket in the close quarters.

“It’s too hot in here,” he exclaimed, folding his coat over his arms. The men otherwise stood in silence. The air was full of tension. Nac ground his teeth. The man in the middle turned and looked over his shoulder at Nac. His face was stoic. His eyes dismissive. He stepped back, bumping into Nac’s shoulder again.

The door opened. The three men stepped out into the hallway of the twelfth floor. Nac let out a sigh and looked at Vine, who shook his head to indicate they should remain inside. The doors closed and the elevator began to rise again. Reaching the thirteenth floor the doors opened with a chime and both men stepped into the hallway. They turned toward unit 1314.

After a quick walk down the light blue carpeted hallway they arrived at a sand colored door, matching all of the others in the corridor. A welcome mat greeted them with a garnet version of the palmetto tree and crescent moon. Vine knocked heavily on the door and waited.

A young man opened the door and looked quizzically at the duo standing in the hallway. He was clean shaven with small pock-marks scattered over his face. He wore a simple brown suit, that seemed just one size too big. "Can I help you?" he asked.

Vine towered over the much smaller man. "We're here to see Marcus," Vine stated. "We're a little early, but he's expecting us."

"Oh, you must be his friends that he said were coming over at eight. I'm glad you're here. I get to go home now."

"Good for you, can you go get the Senator?" Vine asked quickly.

"Sure, umm, one second," the young man hesitated. "Can I take your coats, or-"

A commanding voice emanated from the back room of the apartment. "Ahh, you guys made it." The senator walked slowly around the corner and into view. "Great to see you again. Kyle, why don't you head home to your family. My friends will keep me company for a while. I'll see you at the office tomorrow."

"Yes sir." Kyle quickly walked to the table to grabbed his coat.

"Why don't you fellas come inside and let's talk. I have a few good bottles of wine we can enjoy."

"See you tomorrow, sir." Kyle brushed past Nac and Vine as they stepped inside. He closed the door on his way out. Vine quickly locked it behind him.

The apartment was big for D.C. standards of the time.

The room was simple, but the walls were covered with military mementos ranging from shadow boxes of flags to framed photos of operational units. Nac's primary focus was the chandelier above the small table. It was an A-10 Thunderbolt II in full nose dive. The gatling gun had been augmented. Each barrel held a light supported by random inches of illuminated piping, creating a circular glow of tracer rounds brightening the room.

"I hope you drink." Marcus turned to face the two men, holding a bottle of red wine in his hand. "It's a Pinot Noir from the Revana vineyard in Napa Valley. I try to keep it American when I can. American wine is underrated. Too many people focus on proving they know wine, instead of just enjoying a good glass."

Vine smiled widely. "I like a good red. I don't know much. My old Major was in training to become a sommelier when he wasn't stacking bodies. After he went down, we all added to our repertoire. Hedonism has many forms."

"Have a seat, gentlemen. Get me up to speed." Marcus stated, walking to the table.

Nac and Vine sat at the table as Marcus came over with three glasses and a bottle. Nac leaned over and whispered, "Vine, for a love of wine?"

Vine looked to Nac and nodded, smiling a toothy yellowy white smile.

"So, gentlemen, what's going on here? The police tell me they think it's a terrorist attack targeting the banks."

"They're right and wrong, sir," Vine replied.

"Don't call me sir."

"Nac and I, my name's Vine by the way, are members of a time travelling agency known as The Bulwark. The future for mankind is bleak. No matter what we do, mankind has a definite end, at least to life as you know it."

Vine paused and took a sip of his wine.

"Originally, the Saharan Bloodbath of the twenty-second century led to radical Islamists detonating Iranian nukes all over Europe and the Americas. Several countries, not all, responded in kind. It sparked a global nuclear war that killed ninety-nine percent of the Earth's population. Most land was unusable afterwards except for a few remote islands and previously uninhabited deserts. Everything deemed to have strategic value was destroyed. Mankind reverted back to a kind of tribal time. Clean water became the ultimate luxury."

Marcus stared at him. The blood drained from his face. His right hand clenched his wine glass resting on the table. He reached up and ran his left hand through his hair. His fingers trembled.

"In our first campaign, we members of The Bulwark managed to stop the global war. It wasn't easy. At first we tried shifting global politics and creating peace in regions previously devoid of peace. We weren't successful. Too many special interest groups profited from conflict. Too many politicians saw defense as a jobs program. We then set about stopping the Islamist attacks.

"We were mostly successful, but some nukes were still detonated. We did manage to curtail the response and avoid the chain reaction. Unfortunately, New York City, Washington D.C, Moscow, London, Paris, Berlin, Rio De Janiero, Beijing, Hong Kong, and Tel Aviv were unsaveable. The radical Islamists had too many redundancies in place and were aided by the NPs. That was our first encounter with the NPs."

"And who are the NPs?" Marcus interrupted.

"NPs are the New Puritans. They're an offshoot of a

group from this time that you may have heard of, The Westboro Baptist Church. My understanding is that in your time they're seen as a joke, a media headline. Late in the 21st century a man by the name of Fred Sebastian Cole militarized some of the more radical members. They began bombing bars and other locations they deemed filled with 'undesirables.' Their targets mostly included the gay and non-christian communities.

"They grew in power and influence until the global wars. Several key members of the New Puritans survived the bombings. Their location in middle America saved them from the harshest bombardment. They also were survivalists and had already been operating out of deeply buried bunkers. They viewed the nuclear war as a sign of the second coming of Christ. They think our attempts to save mankind are actually denying us Christ's salvation."

"Fucking psychos perverting the good word." Marcus shook his head, wine glass shaking slightly in his hand. "Chop off one head, and another replaces it. These fucks are probably no different than ISIS. Cowards hiding behind scripture are still cowards."

Vine waited for the Senator to finish, then continued. "With the prevention of the chain reaction, after the Saharan Bloodbath ended, relative global peace took over as countries tried to rebuild; however, it was tenuous at best. Resources became tighter and tighter. Consumption spiraled out of control. By the 23rd century, wars were primarily over clean water and access to desert space."

"Why deserts?"

"Most habitable land was fully developed with large cities and dense populations of people. Even some smaller deserts had been fully settled. Solar power was the leading form of electricity. Equatorial desert locations became prime real estate for the leading power companies. Countries even went to war to secure access to the areas. In this time, people battle over the land for oil. In the future, it's for sunlight. The Sahara Desert became one of the most highly sought after locations. It was also the site of some of the bloodiest battles."

Marcus sighed and shook his head. "I went to war for my country during the first Gulf War. I've watched both of my sons go to war in the Global War on Terror. Are you telling me we we're still fighting over the same land?"

Vine paused and took a drink of his wine. He swished it around in his slightly open mouth and breathed in. In spite of the darkness of the conversation, a bit of joy appeared on his face. "You can imagine it's hard to find good wine with real estate being such a tight commodity in the future," he said. "Your fight wasn't a lost cause. The Marshall Plan was duplicated by the United Nations in much of the Middle East late in the twenty first century. The region actually became a thriving commercial area for a few years."

"Okay, so it's not all bleak, right? And, if you're saying humanity has reached new levels of population, that means you succeeded, right?" Marcus asked.

"We did for a time. Late in the 23rd century more wars broke out over water. They were vicious. It all started in 2376. China was in crisis. Due to all of the pollution from the previous three hundred years, there was no clean water left for its people. It solved the problem with Nepal. China conquered Nepal in a matter of days, killing over fifty million Nepalis, and diverted the Kosi, Gandaki, and Karnali rivers inland. These river systems were still pure as they originated from the few remaining Himalayan glaciers. They also were the main tributaries for the Ganges river.

Unfortunately, this meant India lost most of one of its major sources of water. The Ganges was also sacred to the Hindus of India. India responded with a full invasion of southwest China and Nepal. The result was the bloodiest war in human history. It's known as The War of the Elephants. Over five billion people lost their lives in the opening throes of the land war.

"Allies from all sides were pulled in for support. The NPs used this to their advantage and began detonating nukes in key locations. We tried to stop them, but it was no use. Each time we foiled one bombing, they simply blew up a different city. With political tensions so high, the slightest spark could cause a wildfire. A nuke, well, you can imagine the result. In the end, over twenty two billion more people died, and we were left with a nearly uninhabitable planet once again." Nac noted that Vine's voice became more agitated as he talked about the horrors ahead.

"So, let me get this straight, India got pissed that someone fucked with its water sources? Makes sense."

"It was during this time we realized, no matter what we do, we're merely stationary defenses. We take ground, the NPs analyze and re-engage with the benefit of hindsight. After several costly battles, we decided to open a new front."

"This prompted our second campaign. We began conducting psyops, or a war for the minds of humanity. We released thousands of books and movies throughout time trying to spur people into action. Our thought was, if China can maintain its clean water, the whole war can be averted."

"Anything I might know?" Marcus asked.

"Definitely. Have you heard of Superman?"

"You guys wrote Superman?" Marcus asked skeptically.

"Not entirely, but we did give Jerry Siegel the idea that Krypton was destroyed by excessive use of its planetary resources. It didn't make it into all of the lore, but nuclear chain reactions and planetary overconsumption are themes present in many tellings of Krypton's demise. We've had writers work on projects ranging from comics to novels, movies to commercials. The goal was to reach everyone. We wanted everyone to understand that protecting our resources is the key to peace.

"A few of our titles from your time in the United States include The Day After Tomorrow, Tomorrow Never Dies, The Hunger Games, Fallout the original video game, and the Daisy spot in the 1964 presidential election. I don't know all of our titles. Those are just the few that I liked."

"How about Twelve Monkeys or Contagion?" Marcus asked, getting up to open another bottle of wine.

"Viral issues have never been the cause of total destruction. There was the Green Death in the late twenty-first century. No one knows exactly how it started, but in dense Brazilian slums on the outskirts of Sao Paolo the plague spread like wildfire in a draught. It killed roughly half of the human population on Earth. However, since the land was still arable, humanity recovered."

Marcus made the rounds as he listened, refilling the men's drinks.

"To the future," Marcus raised his glass as he sat down.

Vine shared the toast and took a sip. The look of bliss returned to his face as he paused. The three men sat in silence for a moment, taking in the peace of the room and the harmony of the wine.

Marcus broke the silence. "What was Wayne working on with you? How can I help?"

"We're currently starting another new campaign. Wayne was one of several major banking leaders we had recruited. We had Wayne with Goldman Sachs. We also recruited top executives, sometimes more than one, at many other leading banks ranging from Bank of America and Deutsche Bank to Barclays and Nomura Holdings. We need this to be a global effort. Each recruit must not only get his or her respective bank on board, but also help in the lobbying effort for political support. It's a monumental task."

"And what exactly is the end goal?"

"We're creating a specialized mutual fund called the Human Fund. I heard the name has ties to a popular American television show in the 1990's titled 'Seinfeld'. Players must divert ten percent of all investments given to the bank into this mutual fund. So, if Nac here buys ten thousand dollars of Apple stock, he actually receives nine thousand dollars of Apple, and one thousand dollars of the human fund. The performance of this fund will be tied to measures of global peace, access of education, food, clean water, medical care, and other measures you all determine. We want your input in creating the perfect fund. We hope to have the United Nations set up a meter with their analysis of each factor and preside over any adjustments in fund value."

"Wow, that's ambitious," Marcus replied. "You're trying to tie ten percent of global wealth to the performance of mankind?"

"Correct," Vine stated. He relaxed in his chair and

took another sip. “It will need political support to keep the fund afloat. However, if it works, pollution levels may decrease to the point where the Chinese may never need to divert water from India in the first place. Each country in the world may have more wealth, and increased prosperity. That’s the objective. Sound like something you want to be a part of?”

“How can I say no to that?"

“Good, we’ll assign you protection as well. With the NP activity targeting Wayne, we’re taking it as a sign of encouragement. They wouldn’t have killed him if his actions were pointless. Keep that as motivation. You will be successful."

Chapter 4

Several hours later

"So," Marcus paused, "These ants?"

"Automated news telecasts," Vine replied.

"Triggered the what again?" He asked.

"War of the Molehill."

Marcus cocked his head sideways, clutching a mostly empty bottle firmly in his right hand. He hesitantly opened his mouth as another China Cat Sunflower riff ended. "Is he making this up?"

"I'm new," Nac smiled. "No idea." He sat back and relaxed.

"It was in the 23rd Century. Greece was nearly debt free. An Ottomon heritage march was confronted by a few teenage Nazi wannabes in Athens. Rocks were thrown. A knife was pulled. No one was hurt. In reality, some morons squared up and walked away without ever throwing a punch. Two people had minor wounds from light trampling. If they'd been tough, they'd've walked away. By the time the news broke, it was a full scale race brawl.

"Apparently there were enough key words in the headlines that the banks news parsing and machine learning bots expected a negative shock to the economy, triggering a global selloff.

"Sounds like just another bit of cyclical recessions to me," Marcus leaned forward.

"Greece was unable to handle it and plummeted into another cycle of depression. Citizens fled to Albania, Macedonia, and Bulgaria. Turkey wasn't as welcoming. The area had so many catastrophes, people were no longer called refugees. They were renamed nomads. Turkey stopped accepting nomads. Tensions rose over time. Bombs went off. War broke out. After a few billion dead, someone blew a whistle."

"And it was called the Molehill War? Why?" Marcus asked.

"A fight over a fiction?" Nac interjected.

"You mean The Crusades? Wayne always called them the battle of the sky wizards," Marcus laughed. "Was there ever a war of the unicorns?"

Nac perked up in his chair, eyes having been mostly shut. His right eye opened wide but his left stayed half closed. Vine simply shook his head, then finished his glass. "Well, Marcus, I think we need to get going." Vine looked to the counter with four empty bottles of wine. "It'll be around nine in the morning when we get back, so this is technically day drinking for us.

"Also, as a little motivation, I'll talk to our boss about taking you to control so you can see what it looks like. If he approves it, I'll give you a little tour. Want to check it out?"

Marcus stood and shook Vine's hand. "Definitely, and thank you. I was distressed enough when I thought my children were finishing the fight in Iraq that my generation started. To think their children will still have the same fight for the next hundred years is unacceptable. I'll do my part to ensure that doesn't happen."

He moved to Nac and shook his hand. He placed his left hand on Nac's shoulder. "I'm sorry about what happened to your teammates."

"Nac, come over here and let's jump home," Vine called from across the room. Nac quickly joined the larger man at the center of the living space.

Nac picked up his backpack, noting its extra weight as he readied to return to headquarters. He keyed in his wristband and watched as both his band and Vine's turned green.

"See you fellas later," Marcus stated with a wave and a smile.

"Don't forget to clench," Vine reminded.

In a flash the room changed from the simple DC apartment to the sterile white walls of The Bulwark main operating center. Nac grimaced, squinting his eyes and focusing on the floor, hands on his knees. He swallowed his cough, and smiled. He slowly stood upright.

Alum strode to the platform with her medical kit. Nac looked around and saw Griz, Dr. G, and Diana at the base of the launch point. Diana lowered her gaze. A small smile appeared on her face as she bit her lip for a moment, wrapping her hands around her stomach and grabbing her hips, then glancing back up.

Alum approached Vine first and scanned each of his eyes, pausing for a second in confusion. "Are you drunk?" she asked, exasperatedly.

"No, mind your own business." Vine replied. Red stains on his normally white teeth revealed their past few hours of libations. Alum shook her and and began to scan Nac.

"Glad you took your first mission so seriously." Dr. G. barked from behind Alum.

"They're both clean," Alum stated with a hint of venom in her tone. She turned and walked down the two steps to the main floor. She didn't look back until she came to a halt beside Dr. G. She whispered something in his ear, causing him to tilt his head. His hand rose for a moment as though to wipe his mouth but stopped after only a twitch.

"We were successful in our mission, sir. The senator is a great host. I haven't had wine like that since, ever, but don't tell him that," Vine stated. His face appeared softer, and his eyes warm and happy. The two men stepped down from the launch point. Vine stumbled on the bottom step but regained his footing. He glanced around sheepishly, hoping no one had noticed then moved to the original command console with a toothy red smile. "I guess I'm out of practice."

"Anyways, if you two want to stop judging, we brought you something. Or, Nac and I can keep it to ourselves." Each man reached into their bag and pulled out a bottle.

Alum's eyes lit up and she grabbed the bottle from Nac, while Vine casually reached out and handed his to the excited Doctor. She whispered in Dr. G.'s ear again as she walked past, causing the older man to clear his throat and cock his head. She placed the bottles in a previously unnoticed hideous orange bag at the base of the command console.

"Now, if you two want to stop, whatever that was, we can get down to work," Vine snarked. "Marcus is going to recruit banking leaders and obtain political backing, specifically IMF leaders. I think he's going to be a real asset."

"I've never met anyone as genuine as he was," Nac added. "When you talk to him, he's focusing on your words, and makes you the complete center of his attention. He somehow puts you completely at ease. He seems to truly care about others. I wish I'd voted for him now."

"I want him protected even as a child. We know what the NPs are willing to do. Marcus is one of us now. He deserves the best," Dr. G. stated.

"We already have at least twenty volunteers for long term missions. I'll go through them and pick out the best candidates," Diana added. "Do you have anyone you definitely want on the mission?"

"No. Give me names and I'll go through them. Can you have them ready in an hour?"

"Yes sir."

"Anything else you two noticed about the mission that I should be aware of? Any additional information?" Diana asked looking to Nac and Vine.

"No. It was straight-forward," Vine replied. "I'd like to take Marcus and Nac to control. I think it might help put things in perspective."

"Okay, why don't you two turn in your gear and sober up. I'd like you to be here tomorrow for the protection missions. We plan to start at 0800. Pre-brief at 0700 if you want to attend that. If all goes well tomorrow, I'll think about approving your request."

Nac and Vine grabbed their packs and walked down the hallway toward the armory as Diana began her mission preparations.

The next morning Nac groaned as he heard a sharp

knock at the door. He rolled to his side and buried his face under the pillow. “Go away!" he bellowed weakly at the door.

The knock was repeated. Nac peeked out from under his pillow and saw the time: 0630. He looked toward the door and saw the screen displaying his guest, Diana. He rolled up to a seat and groaned, holding his stomach. His mouth was parched, and his lips were dry as sandpaper. He stood, cleared his throat. “One second,” he said to the door as he grabbed the jeans from a ball on the floor. He opened the door widely and stepped into the threshold to be greeted by a snort.

“You look terrible," she said. “I thought you might need a little help this morning, so I brought you some coffee."

“Thanks," Nac replied, accepting the small white cup. He took a sip and his eyes grew wide as the coffee burned his tongue and tasted similar to that served fondly by the cooks on Guadalcanal, day seventy five.

“How is it?" Diana asked, curling the end of her hair with her fingers while she stood in the doorway.”

“Great, thanks.” Nac replied, blinking back a tear and taking another sip.

“I don’t actually drink but I’m told coffee helps.”

“You’re right, I don’t feel my hangover anymore. Care to come inside?”

“No, I have work to do, but I’m sure you’ll find a friend before too long. After all, that’s what you al--”

Nac glanced up in confusion as she trailed off.

Diana cleared her throat and glanced up “Don’t worry. This isn’t the first time someone’s drank on a mission. Recruitment can go lots of ways. Dr. G. may be hard on you today, but he just wants you to be solid when he needs you."

Nac ran his free left hand through his hair and rubbed his stubbly face, peeking out at Diana from between his fingers. She stood in one inch burgundy flats. Her athletic legs disappeared under a floral print white sundress. Her hair was a vibrant blonde, streaming down her back from the tight constraints of a headband.

"Did you do something new with your hair?" Nac asked.

"Yes, I like to mix it up from time to time. I even used to have purple streaks when I was younger. If you thought the tailor was high tech, the salon will blow you away. You should check it out."

"Am I out of style?"

"No, and please don't get a haircut like Griz." She smiled at him until he took another sip of his coffee. He steeled himself before it bit. "Well, I need to go get ready for the pre-brief. You may want to skip it, to, clean up. Try to be in the ops center at eight to see us in action. I think it'll be interesting for you to see how we work. You and Vine are only one of several teams we have working. I don't get days off like you two do." She added, already beginning to walk away.

Nac quickly turned back inside and placed the coffee onto the nightstand. As the door closed, Nac swaddled himself in the heavy grey wool comforter.

He remained in bed for a solid thirty minutes before finally dragging himself back from under the warmth of his blankets. He chugged a glass of water and immediately dropped to the floor for his morning ritual. Six sun salutations later, he regained his footing and opened his closet to the bright colors inside.

After pulling on an undershirt he grabbed a black

shirt with pink paisley pattern, and threw it to the ground, shaking his head. He next grabbed a plain white button up and quickly slipped it on, along with a soft red cashmere v-neck sweater. Pulling on a pair of jeans, black belt and shoes, he walked to the mess hall.

The room was easily the size of a football field. Small tables, all with drab grey tops and metal legs, dotted the area. To the far right side he saw several equally bland sofas with smaller coffee tables. On the left wall were many low tables with only cushions for seats. A pleasant aroma tickled his nostrils, filling the air, filtering in from the back side of the cavernous room.

People were dressed erratically, from classic suits and ties to neon tights, from polyester to silk, everything could be seen. There were close to a thousand people devouring their food. The assorted dining stations were at least half full of patrons. Nac took his position at the end of the line. It moved quickly, and within a few minutes he was at the front. He grabbed a tray and stepped to the first station.

He grabbed premade items in styrofoam containers. Within sixty seconds he'd fully loaded his tray, and walked farther down the line. Nac grabbed a cornbread, yogurt parfait, and several strips of bacon. Moving farther he reached a wall of coolers full of drinks. Some looked familiar, Coca Cola, skim milk, and root beer. Others looked outlandish. Neon holograms depicting strange scenes adorned bottles of liquids in various colors. He grabbed two cartons of milk and one bottle with an eye catching logo, a five second holographic video loop of a girl in a bikini guzzling from the bottle, pausing to smile at the end. The fluid inside was a dark brown color.

Finished loading up, he headed out to the main dining area and spotted Vine sitting at a table near the middle of the room talking with several others. Nac walked over to the table and stood across from Vine.

"Mind if I join you?"

"You look like roadkill shit."

Nac placed his tray on the table. "I didn't see a bloody mary station in line, but I guess they have everything else. I swear, I need an IV. Vine, Fuck you."

Vine indicated the other two companions at the table. "This is Burns, and this is Erish."

They exchanged introductions briefly as Nac looked at the two. Burns was slightly whiter than his sun softened golden graphic tee shirt. He was out of shape, yet his tee was just a bit too small with too much bedazzling. His dirty blond hair was excessively gelled back and meticulously controlled without a single strand out of place.

Erish couldn't have been more striking. Her rich black hair was perfectly smooth. Her dress was soft pink in color with white accents. Her dark skin had no blemishes. Even her eyebrows looked effortlessly immaculate. With her dark brown eyes she gazed deeply at Nac as he sat down. Nac met her eyes and was mesmerized for a moment. He blushed as he stole his gaze away.

"This is Nac, the guy I was telling you about. Nac, Burns and Erish are volunteering to help with the senator."

"Nice to meet you guys," Nac stated.

"I hear you were recruited just the other day. How are you settling in?"

"So far so good. I spent a few hours at the polybox yesterday and got some decent clothing. I also made a few bad decisions. Never drink and tailor," he added with a sarcastic grin.

"I hear Griz is jealous of you," Burns stated, receiving a sharp look from Erish.

"Why's that?"

"He's been here since he was a kid. He's always looked up to the field agents. Then, well, you can guess what happens then.

"No, I can't."

"They disappear. Agents don't usually last long, even since Dr. G. took over," Erish answered.

"Anyways, he's always wanted to be a field agent, but he's better off helping out here. With Vine not having a partner for a while, he was hoping to take the job, but it looks like you've filled in," Burns finished.

Nac frowned and glanced down at his food, poking it with his fork.

"Yeah, he's a good kid, but as green as they come," Vine interjected. "Besides, until he passes Grom's basic weapons tests, it's a waste of breath.

Nac shrugged. "What tests? I didn't take any tests."

"Thanks for reminding me," Vine replied.

"So, I don't get it. How're agents disappearing. We got those bands, right?" Nac broke the silence.

"Yes, I've heard a rumor that they somehow disable our countermeasures. We don't exactly know how, but Griz is working on a solution."

"Why Griz? Isn't he like twelve?"

"He's a certifiable genius for one," Burns answered. "And even though we aren't supposed to talk about our past, everyone knows his story."

"When he got here he was so young," Erish interjected. "I think he was only eight, and his sister Arwen was maybe four. Even though he'd just lost his parents, he focused solely on his sister. Maybe it was his coping mechanism. Regardless, he was so nurturing to her, never asking for help, that everyone fell in love with him. We've all watched him grow up."

"As for his role in operations, he's from the twenty-fifth century, just before the last collapse. He grew up with technology we can only dream of. So, he has the best knowledge. Since he grew up around our operations, he's always wanted to help out. I don't even think it's for revenge. He's just genuinely a good person. His dream since as long as I can remember is to be a field agent, but I don't think he's left the compound since he arrived over ten years ago. He used to follow Rana around whenever he could, mimicking her every move, trying to be like her," Burns added.

Vine's head jerked upright and his smile faded. "Okay okay, careful guys. You know the rules. How many new redwoods have been hung on the wall since you got here? We're in trouble if I'm the one keeping us in line. Anyways, we need to head to the operations center in a few minutes," Vine stated, pointing to the large clock on the wall, digitally displaying the time, 0750.

Nac nodded and held the neon bottle up, popping open the resealable top. Everyone looked at him strangely. Not noticing, he took a sip, and for a split second his face contorted in a combination of pain and disgust. He opened his mouth repeatedly like a dog eating peanut butter. "That was terrible."

Vine laughed. "I could have told you that," he said.

"What is it?"

"It's called Diet Sweep. It was supposed to be a similar experience to tasting chocolate-covered bacon; salty, then sweet, but I think the designers screwed up. Even the regular version is crap."

"Ugh," he groaned. "I wanted to try a new item each day to explore the options. Clearly that was a bad call," Nac stated, wiping his mouth and placing the still mostly full bottle back onto the tray.

The group stood, walked to a nearby trash receptacle and emptied their trays. Food and styrofoam alike, as soon as it entered the trash basin, all broke down into pellets. The pellets continually decreased in size until disappearing into the bottom of the dark trash bin. A discoloration in the air above the basin revealed a waft of steam.

Nac glanced around and saw the trio already walking to the exit. He ripped a napkin in half and dropped it into the bin. He noted where it began to pelletize, then quickly poked his left pointer finger in and out once. He raised his hand to his face and examined his digit. Pristine. He smiled, and jogged after the group, already approaching the exit.

They walked to the operations center. Vine took the lead, followed by Erish and Burns, softly clasping one another's hands, with Nac in the rear. When they reached the operations center they moved to the control console at the base of the launch point. Dr. G, Diana, and Griz stood near the main operations table with four other individuals nearby.

"Well, well, well, you two made it after all," Dr. G stated to Nac and Vine with a hint of condescension as the group arrived. He smiled, and for the first time Nac didn't despise the older man. "I'm surprised you didn't keep the fun going all day and night." It returned quickly.

"Next time," Nac replied looking toward Dr. G, wearing his customary white short sleeve silk button up shirt, powder blue shorts, and sandals. Griz came into full view from behind Dr. G. wearing his usual monocle readout with long brown spikes poking out the top. Otherwise, he was dressed in a white dress shirt with ten button navy blue vest in two vertical rows of five. A gold chain dangled from a button on his sternum and disappeared into a pocket above his right hip. His pants were a golden yellow and tied off below the knees, but above white socks and large black shoes with at least a two inch thick sole.

"Just so long as you know when to work and when to play, that's all I care about," Diana interjected while looking around the room. "Where are Milo and Davan?"

"We're here!" Nac heard from behind him and spun around.

Two tall men hurried in from the hallway and joined the group. Both were dressed in extremely sleek dark charcoal suits with dark black dress shoes, capped toes polished to a high sheen. They also both had jet black hair and slightly olive toned skin. They each looked to be in their early thirties, but the man on the left appeared a little younger.

"Are you two ready to get going?" Diana asked. "You're up first."

"Let's do it," the older man nodded.

Vine walked over and shook the hand of the man in grey. "Looking sharp, Milo! Who're you trying to fool?"

"Hey man, at least in the past I won't have to listen to your shit. Besides, we want to make a good first impression. Hopefully the ladies will think this is a genuine GGG suit."

"Good luck," Vine replied with a laugh, slapping Milo

on the shoulder. "You'll need all the help you can get."

The two men walked over to the main platform and grabbed a few backpacks with gear as Griz moved over to the main console.

Nac joined Griz at the transport station and leaned into his ear, "What's going on? I missed the pre-brief this morning."

"The usual for you? Clearly you're perfect for the job," Griz replied with a scowl. He took an overdramatic breath. "They've broken the protection mission for the senator into four groups in twenty year segments. Milo and Davan have drawn first watch from 1950 to 1970."

"But he wasn't even born until 1962. Why so early?" Nac interrupted.

"The NPs have been known to take out targets without discretion. Sometimes they go to the very point of birth. Other times they just kill someone's parents before they're born. We need to cover all of our bases. Their mission isn't true protection. It's just to alert us to any NP activity should it arise. Then, we send in a team of field agents to handle the real fight."

"Why would anyone volunteer for a twenty year assignment?"

"Usually it's people who want a change while still helping the cause. Milo and Davan have been here since they were kids. I think Milo was ten years old, and Davan was only six when they got here. Their parents were agents who died in the first campaign. They want to live. The other six are couples and want to get married and start a family away from all of this. They can give their children a normal life if they take the mission. It's a great compromise."

Nac watched as the two men checked their gear one

last time and nodded to Griz. Holding his hand up, Griz began a countdown.

3,

2,

1,

He lowered his hand to engage the jump console. The two men in suits instantly vanished.

“At least one ofthem should be back in thirty seconds to check in. Depending on how many check ins, we may go straight to the next group. Arjuno and Bee are taking 1970 to 1990. Erish and Burns are taking 1990-2010. Snowflake and Unicorn are taking 2010 to 2030.”

Nac looked at the small group of people awaiting their mission. One man and three women stood talking with Burns and Erish. Two of the women were dressed casually, jeans, running shoes, and t-shirts. The other woman was dressed in a simple light blue wrap dress while the man was wearing dark jeans and a matching jean jacket, unbuttoned over a plain white t-shirt.

“How many check ins are exp--”

“Welcome back!" Nac heard from Dr. G. and looked up. Milo stood tall on the platform dressed in blue jean bell bottom pants, an psychedelic tie dye print button up shirt, red lensed round glasses, and a giant grin. His hair had a few flecks of grey, and he appeared to be about ten pounds heavier than a moment ago. “Did you come straight from Woodstock?"

“No, but we’re looking forward to going in a few years. We just wanted to report that the first decade went smoothly. No issues for his parents. They just got married, and without any involvement, the baby senator should be born in two more years. I have to say, his mom lived in San Francisco, and I’m glad I got that assignment.

San Francisco in the 1950's is something you all have to experience."

"I'll take that under advisement. Thanks for checking in. We'll see you in another decade," Dr. G. replied. "Stay out of trouble."

"Will do. Send me back, Griz."

Griz held up his hand in countdown once again.

3,

2,

1,

He pressed the console again. Nac watched as Milo vanished into thin air.

Dr. G. turned around, laughing. "Maybe we all should take a field trip one day to some of these exotic locations I keep seeing you all enjoy your missions so much. I'm getting jealous."

"You mean your trips to control aren't exotic?" Vine asked.

"Hopefully one day they will be."

"Or we could add some color to this place," Alum interjected. "The decor isn't exactly warm and welcoming here. Maybe we could even have a celebration of our own so everyone can join in,"

"Great idea," Diana agreed, failing to hide a smile.

"Not a bad idea. Look into it when you have some free time," Dr. G. acquiesced.

Alum rolled her eyes. She and the younger Diana smiled at each other as Milo and Davan reappeared. Milo appeared to have gained at least forty more pounds. His former black hair was streaked with grey and a he bore a matching salt and pepper beard and mustache.

He turned toward the main room, revealing his tight blue jeans were topped by a tucked in button up paisley shirt, unbuttoned from his neck to his sternum. A large golden chain dangled from his neck displaying a peace sign. Davan appeared about the same as before. His hair was still jet black, yet grown out into shoulder-length unkempt look. Otherwise he was wearing a polyester blue suit with red dress shirt. His large red collar popped out atop the blue suit. His shoes were black with a gloss matching his hair.

"Hey, guys. Wow, this has been a great assignment," Milo stated. "Hilton Head Island has been the perfect place for me to start a family. The senator is fine. He's seven and a half now and doing great. No NP activity detected at all."

Alum quickly ascended the stairs and performed her medical check on each man. "Your cholesterol levels are a bit high. Lay off the Southern fried foods and sweet tea and you should be fine. Otherwise, you check out just fine."

The two men stepped down from the launch point. "We both would like to return to our assignment where we left. It's been an honor to help, but we really have something great going where we are. Hilton Head is a dream come true for me."

"Definitely," Dr. G. stated. "You both should be proud of the difference you have made. You've been a great help, and we wish you nothing but the best in the future." He walked over and shook each man's hand to congratulate them. "Do you need anything to help you when you get back or are the funds in your accounts still fine?"

"We're good," Milo answered, with a large smile. "We're definitely good."

"Outstanding. Naturally, we need you to help get Arjuno and Bee oriented on their mission. Then your service is complete. Davan, what's your plan?"

"Hilton Head isn't for me. I plan to go to New York City, find a nice spot in Manhattan, and have some fun. These last few years on the island have been brutally boring. Half of my time is spent babysitting his kids." He shrugged to Milo. "I'm looking forward to replacing pacifiers with strippers and blow."

Nac laughed. "I'll be sure to visit."

The two men headed over to the two casually dressed women and shared a few stories, family photos, and hugs.

"Great start today. One down, three to go. Hopefully everything goes this smoothly. Bee, Arjuno, are you two ready?" Dr. G. asked.

"Yes," they replied in unison.

"Okay, let's keep this moving. Milo, Davan, Bee, Arjuno, head up to the platform," he commanded.

Milo and Davan exchanged final hugs with the women, then proceeded to join the couple on the elevated platform. As they walked by Vine, Milo stopped and gave him a big hug. "Thanks for everything."

"No problem. Maybe I'll pop into Hilton Head sometime and visit. I just can't believe you tricked some Southern girl into dating you."

"Not just date, but get married. I have three kids!" He raised his left ring finger up to display a small golden band.

"That poor woman." Vine replied cheerfully. Milo then turned and joined the other three on the platform.

"Ready?" Griz asked.

All four members nodded in reply. Griz held his hand up.

3,

2,

1,

He pressed the button on the jump console and the group vanished. Dr. G. turned around. "Burns, Erish, are you ready? I want to keep this moving along."

"We're ready and excited. Between Hilton Head, Columbia, Tampa, and Washington D.C. I think we have an exciting twenty years ahead of us," Burns replied, clasping Erish's left hand between both of his palms. Nac looked to Diana, who was plotting out the current mission timeline on the large plastic screen. She leaned forward, her bright blonde hair cascaded over her shoulders hiding her face from his gaze.

"Naturally you won't be involved in his deployment to Saudi Arabia during the Gulf War, but otherwise, keep a close eye on him. If anything happens in that deployment or any other time, let us know."

"Will do sir," Burns replied.

"We plan to start a family as soon as we get there," Erish added, clasping Burn's hand more tightly. "That way they won't be infants when we have our first big move. We thi--"

"They should be back by now," Griz interrupted. "It's been thirty five seconds." Alum rushed to a workstation near the back of the room.

Silence fell over the room as everyone waited for the sixty second emergency timer. Erish began to cry. Burns pulled her into his chest. One of his hands gently rubbed her back as she pressed her face into his chest.

"Forty seconds."

The two women who Nac realized must be Snowflake and Unicorn stepped a little closer together and hugged. Unicorn turned to Snowflake and wrapped her arms around her body, hands clasped tightly at Snowflakes left bicep. She rested her head on Snowflake's shoulder.

"Forty five seconds. If the emergency countermeasure kicked in, they'll be here at sixty."

Alum rushed to the launch point, burdened with a large white case. It had a large red cross emblazoned on the top. A whimper escaped from Erish, face still buried in Burns' chest. He continued to rub her back gently, trying to soothe her. Her body spasmed with her tears.

"Fifty five."

Erish turned her tear-stained face toward the platform. Burns held her close. Alum's gaze darted between the launch point and Dr. G.

"Sixty seconds," Griz stated.

No one appeared. Burns squeezed his eyes closed and he rested his chin on top of Erish's head. Her body heaved as she cried into his burly body. Soft moans and whimpers emanated from their embrace. Snowflake and Unicorn turned to the platform, still holding one another. Snowflake grabbed Unicorn's arms and held tight.

"Sixty five."

The platform remained empty.

Chapter 5

"Okay, we need to send someone to thirty seconds after they arrive in Hilton Head in 1970. We need Arjuno and Bee to report in at least once a year until whatever the problem is occurs. If it's NP involvement we'll keep decreasing the check in cycles until we get an exact time. Then we can activate you two," Dr. G nodded to Nac and Vine.

"I'll go!" Griz chimed in. "Let me go and give them the update. It makes sense to send me because then I can adjust Bee and Arjuno's transport times to compensate."

"That makes sense," Diana chimed in. "We don't want them returning at the same time, and he's best suited to make the tech adjustment."

"Okay, Griz, you've never jumped before. Don't screw around out there. Just jump, give them the update, and jump back. I want them checking in every year on the dot, you got me?"

"Yes sir!" Griz stated, grinning ear to ear. He reached into a drawer at the launch console and removed a transport control wristband, typed a few inputs, and slid it over his wrist. The wristband immediately turned green. "Ready!" His massive smile remained plastered on his face.

Dr. G. sighed. "Forgetting something?"

"Oh" Griz nodded and walked to the transport platform. Diana took his place behind the console. He removed his visor and placed it in his pocket.

She held up her hand and counted down.

3,

2,

1,

Griz vanished.

"Why do we need the launch point? We jumped from the senator's house yesterday. We've jumped from an alley. Is it really necessary?" Nac asked.

"It's to make jumping orderly," Dr. G. replied sternly. "You return exactly where you left. This way we don't have people jumping into you while you stand there watching us work. It'll happen sometime when you jump to a new place. You may land right on top of someone, or in a crowd, and it's unpleasant. Try explaining it to a random person in a park when you appear on top of them. It's the same reason we space out returns by thirty seconds. We don't want to risk any easily preventable errors, and we don--"

Griz reappeared on the platform, beaming with excitement. "Mission was successful!" he stated, still looking like a kid at christmas.

"First time leaving the compound since you got here Griz?" Vine asked.

"Yeah, almost twelve years," he answered while stepping down from the platform. Alum stopped him in his tracks when he reached the landing. He looked at her with surprise as she indicated the instrument in her hand. His face changed from confusion to understanding, and he nodded as she raised it to each eye quickly.

"You're good," she stated. Griz walked back to the transport console and Diana moved to the side, giving Griz back his spot. "Don't forget to take off your transport band," Dr. G. added. Griz frowned and removed it, placing it back into the drawer where it came from.

A few moments later Arjuno appeared on the platform wearing khaki pants and a classic navy blue polo shirt with dark brown shoes. "Year one is good," he stated. He clenched and unclenched his left hand almost continuously.

"Keep on alert. We'll keep doing annual check-ins until something bad happens. Then we'll move to weekly."

"See you next year," he added. Griz held up his hand.

3,

2,

1,

Arjuno disappeared again.

Dr. G. turned to Nac and Vine. "We're going to iterate through each year until we have an issue, then go to weekly check-ins to isolate a one week operating window for you two. Go get gear from the armory and some clothing for a possible week-long mission. Remember, this is Hilton Head Island in the 1970s."

Nac and Vine walked off to get prepared while Griz, Diana, and Dr. G. continued through quick jumps with Arjuno and Bee. As they left the room they heard Arjuno arrive again. Nac peeked over his shoulder before entering the hallway to see Arjuno, wearing nantucket red shorts, sandals, and a plain white polo shirt.

Thirty minutes later, Nac and Vine walked back into the control room carrying a large duffel bag apiece. The two men were each wearing khaki pants with brown shoes and colorful polo shirts.

"Perfect timing," Griz stated. "We've isolated the issue down to the week of the 4th of July 1975. The senator should be twelve and a half years old then. If I were to guess, the 4th of July being this week isn't a coincidence. The 4th falls on a Friday in 1975, so we're sending you in on Wednesday July second. Take the time to get situated and get the lay of the land. Arjuno last reported that the Shaw family plan is to watch fireworks on the island at Harbor Town. It's a local spot in the Sea Pines plantation. You can stay with Arjuno and Bee in their guest rooms."

Griz grabbed a small data stick from the clear plastic console and walked to the two men. He held the stick near each of their devices for a moment. "All the information you need is now loaded onto your drives. It includes a map of the area at the time, as well as all key addresses. You shouldn't be missing anything necessary."

Dr. G. stepped up. "We still don't know how they're disabling our emergency safeguards. If you run into any NPs, be careful. We can't afford anything to happen to the two of you at this stage of the operation. Still, try to figure out what they're doing to circumvent our protections. It could save lives in the future."

Both men nodded. They each shouldered their packs and stepped up to the platform. Vine gave a quick nod of affirmation to Griz, who held up his hand.

3,

2,

1,

The cool climate controlled room of the compound changed to hot, humid South Carolina mid summer. Looking around to survey their arrival location, the men saw a small creek running no more than a few feet wide, yet it had carved out at least a thirty foot wide gash into the land. It must have been low tide. Tall marsh grass lined both sides of the creek, rising from soft brown mud that was still damp.

Pools of water dotted the muddy landscape. Tiny fiddler crabs scurried in fear away from the new arrivals and burrowed into holes in the mud. Vine checked his wristband, swatting away the flurry of gnats that began to swarm around the new pair. Nac blinked repeatedly as one small inspect lodged itself in his right eye.

"We're two miles from Arjuno's house. Griz must have messed up our arrival location. He should have sent us straight there. But, at least no one spotted us. Let's get this over with."

Nac nodded and followed Vine down the side of the creek for about two hundred meters, feet sinking into the soft mud with each step. They reached a wide concrete road and looked left at a small bridge breaching the waterway. The wooden bridge rose in an arch. A man stood in the middle of the bridge fishing in one of the deeper pockets of collected water attached to the slow moving stream. A white and blue cooler sat at his feet along with a large golden labrador retriever, mouth agape and tongue hanging out. The dog bore the look only contentment can provide. The cooler had a tattered looking sticker affixed to the side reading "Humphrey 68". A beer rested on the railing beside the fisherman's arm.

Nac and Vine turned right and headed toward the locator on their wristbands. They walked in silence until they reached the first turn. They saw a large marina with hundreds of boats anchored. A few outdoor restaurants scattered the area. A large red and white striped lighthouse sat in the far corner of the harbor overlooking the rest of the marina.

"This must be Harbor Town," Nac stated. "We should come back and check it out after we settle in." Vine only nodded and they continued to march forward. "You know, you need to do a better job of educating people on what they're signing up for."

"What?" Vine replied.

"It's nothing."

"Do you regret joining us?"

"No way. I'm a PJ. Our motto is 'That others may live.' I'm definitely earning my green feet. I'm just still trying to wrap my head around everything. You know, I had a date with a chick who I hadn't fucked shit up with yet."

"I worked with a few PJs before. Baddasses, every fucking one. Are you still qualified?"

"I volunteer with a local rescue team when I'm off duty. I just hate being bored."

The two men continued walking until they reached a traffic circle. A large pond sat to the left of the circle. A few alligators, one five feet long and another ten feet long rested on the grass warming in the summer heat. Nac tapped Vine on the shoulder and gestured to the the large reptiles. Without pause the men crossed the road to keep a safe distance and continued to the circle. As they reached the first exit they followed signs to South Beach.

"Half a mile to go," Vine stated as they exited the circle. Nac looked around at the semi-tropical plants lining the walking path alongside the road. They continued to walk, dodging families on bikes and swatting the pesky gnats away.

After only a few more minutes they reached a small one story building with natural wooden finishes. It's façade was a soft brown with darker brown roofing. Each window was outlined with worn brownish green shutters on the sides. The grass was a vibrant green with half inch thick blades of grass. The soft blades leaned upon one another instead of standing straight up. Pine straw was sparsely scattered atop the lawn. The two men walked to the front of the house and knocked on the door.

"Coming!" a female voice emanated from inside. The sound of gentle footsteps tapped from beyond the door, growing ever louder and closer. The bolt unlocked, and the door swung open revealing Bee with a giant smile. She stood wearing a simple white apron with the words *Eden's Kitchen, all food made with love.* Two wooden spoons added a little spice to the purple lettering. Underneath the apron she had a simple black blouse atop white linen pants. A large bulge below the apron showed she must have been nearly six months pregnant. Her face bore a few wrinkles showing the five years which had passed. Her warm eyes and smile revealed those years were good.

"It's so good to see you two! It's been so long. Come inside and put your stuff down," she said as a small hand appeared at her knee. A head poked out from her right side and looked up at the two men. She leaned down and picked up the small child.

"This is Zach," she said, holding him against her hip. "Let's get you settled in. We have two guest rooms down the hallway." The men stepped inside and looked at the simple Southern home. The foyer led to a main living room area. Toys were scattered haphazardly across the floor. Nac reached down and picked up a yellow toy dump truck. After a brief appraisal, he placed it back to the ground and it gently rolled several inches before coming to a stop.

The smell of delicious baked goods permeated the home. “Make yourself at home," she said and quickly moved into the kitchen as a bell began to ring from within.

Nac and Vine each walked down the hallway and dropped their gear into the guest rooms. They rejoined one another in the hallway and headed to the kitchen. Bee stood near the counter over two trays of sizzling cookies. Zach stood behind her, looking up excitedly with a knowing smile.

“Can I get you guys anything? We have milk, water, beer, and sweet tea.”

“A glass of water would be great," Nac answered. “It's pretty hot out there.”

Bee grabbed a glass and filled it, handing it to Nac. She looked back to Zach. “Wait a few minutes for those to cool, then you can have some. You can only have them if you clean up. Now, go put away your toys." Zach ran off to the far room and immediately got to work bundling up the mess.

“He's cute," Vine stated. “And is that another one on the way I see?"

“Yes, we've been so lucky so far. This is a dream come true,” she smiled contentedly as she looked to Zach hurrying to complete his chore.

“Where's Arjuno?”

“Oh, Brad? We don't go by those old names anymore.

Brad's playing golf with some of his friends at the club. He'll be back anytime now. Also, call me Eden."

Vine smiled. "Eden, huh? Where did you come up with that one?"

"My mother gave it to me," she said with a bright smile. "It's a family name. I'm the fifth Eden in a row." She rubbed her belly "and I think number six will be along soon enough. Besides, it wouldn't work for me to be calling my husband Arjuno down at the country club, now would it?"

"I guess not."

"Are you enjoying life here in Hilton Head?"

"It's perfect here."

"You mean you don't miss the old HQ?"

Eden laughed. "Do you see any grey walls in this house?" Nac looked around noting all of the varied colors in the room. Soft yellow walls complimented a dark blue sofa. Paintings adorned every wall.

"It's definitely an upgrade in terms of decor," he commented. "And you're liking life in the South?"

"Of course! You may have forgotten, but I'm originally from Auburn, Alabama." She answered, her accent seeming to grow stronger as she spoke of her roots. "And the best part is the temperature. I know you think it's hot, but I was originally born in 2240. Summer days in Auburn averaged one hundred twenty to one hundred forty degrees. I remember one summer we had a week over one hundred and forty degrees every day. You couldn't even go outside for more than a few minutes. Here, my children will get to play outside and live a life free of PECs."

"PECs?" Nac asked.

"Personal Environment Controls," Vine chimed in.

"Think of it like a mobile air conditioner for those hot summer days. PEC technology was adapted to create our personal shields." He tapped the black belt buckle on his belt.

The sound of the front door opening caused everyone to turn to the foyer. Zach ran off in that direction. A moment later, Brad rounded the corner carrying Zach in his arms. He threw him up into the air above his head, grabbed him by his legs, and turned him upside-down. Brad lowered him back toward the ground, laying him on his back.

"Vine, Nac, it's good to see you," he graciously stated, then grabbed a cookie and quickly devoured it. He grimaced for a moment. "Tiw ht," he mumbled with cookie still stuck to the inside of his mouth. He kept his mouth open, breathing deeply to try to suck in fresh cool air. A few moments later he swallowed and smiled, then kissed Eden on the cheek. "Have you been waiting for me long?"

"No, we just got here. Eden was telling us that you two are settling in nicely," Nac replied.

"Yeah, we're not looking forward to him leaving in a few years for college. Maybe we can remotely monitor his Academy career from here. What's your plan for figuring out this situation?"

"We're going to spend the next two days surveying the area. We'll be in Harbor Town for the fourth to protect the Shaw family. We want you two to stay home that night. If we don't come back, try to get a readout of what happened and jump back to HQ to give them the update. They can then prevent us from walking into whatever bad stuff happened."

"Relax, do nothing, don't get shot at? I think I can handle that," Brad stated with a grin.

The next two days passed uneventfully. Nac and Vine found the Shaw residence. They used the time to get familiar with the family's current appearances. They scouted out Harbor Town to get a feel for its entrances and exits. The harbor itself served as a natural barrier with no exits in two directions, meaning it would be difficult for anyone to escape.

The Fourth of July finally arrived, and the excitement of the tourists was matched by the nervousness of the team. Eden prepared breakfast for everyone as usual, but something seemed lacking. Vine poked at his meal, barely eating anything. No one spoke over the food.

Leaving the family home, Nac and Vine packed a few items into Brad's car and headed off to get early surveillance of the Shaw family. The day passed normally for the family with no work for the day. Morning was spent at the beach. Young Marcus and his sister then went off to the golf course with their dad. Afterwards, the family got ready and drove to Harbor Town to watch for the fireworks.

Nac and Vine set up voice communication with one another and managed to place a transponder on Marcus. The device enabled them to listen in to anything in his vicinity and have a firm readout of his location at all times. The family had a nice dinner at The Crazy Crab then moved to the center of Harbor Town for some live music.

A large crowd began to gather near the stage. The Shaw family found one of the last open benches to sit on nearby. The stage itself was nothing spectacular. It was an elevated wooden platform with a frail wooden railing.

A massive oak tree served as the primary backdrop.

Its thick limbs were wrapped in gray spanish moss which dangled below. Some strands of moss nearly reached the stage. Sporadic loud explosions rang out in all directions, sometimes accompanied by colorful bursts as individuals set off their own firework celebrations. The harbor itself sat farther behind the stage full of large boats. One massive hundred foot yacht was moored almost directly behind the stage center.

A man walked up to the stage and moved to the center to immediately become surrounded by scores of small children. He took a seat on the bar stool in the middle. He reached down and grabbed his guitar to the roar of applause from the children at his feet. The man plucked the guitar a few times, then stood, letting his guitar rest against the ground. Grabbing the microphone, he began.

“Happy 4th of July everybody." He smiled, looking around the large gathering as everyone cheered. “I’m Greg Russell, and I hope y’all are ready for a great night in Harbor Town!" He paused again as the crowd cheered. “I hope those of you who took part in the Bubble Gum Cruise are still going strong and ready for some good songs and fireworks." A few hoots interrupted him, followed by raucous applause. Small children waved signs, hoping to get noticed. “Let’s get started!"

The man began to sing and the whole of Harbor Town was fixed on his words. Hundreds of children's voices joined in making the sound of song carry above the noise of even sporadic firecracker explosions. Nac and Vine separated, taking up positions on either side of the stage fifty feet away. They could hear and see anyone moving toward the Shaw family. After a few more songs Nac heard a different soft noise in his ear.

"What's that?" he asked.

"Nothing."

"You don't hear that?"

"Nope," came a mumbled reply.

"Are you eating something?"

"No."

"Lying prick."

"Yeah, I got some ice cream. It's hot, don't judge."

"Glad you're staying focused. What kind?" Nac asked, wiping sweat from his forehead and rubbing on his khaki shorts. He felt his Salty Dog Cafe T-shirt was already getting a little soaked with sweat from the summer heat.

"Strawberry and Vanilla."

"Where'd you get it?"

"There's a spot only one hundred feet away toward the parking lot. Don't suffer just because we're on alert. It's not like we see anything suspicious anyway."

"Okay, keep an eye out, I'll be right back."

"What're you getting?"

"The Salted Caramel, and throw some sort of sugar on top." Nac stated while walking toward the nearby ice cream stand. After a moment he strolled back to his post, standing watch over the Shaw family.

As he regained his spot he heard the singer reach a new height in his song.

"Oh, Huff the magic dragon lived by the sea
And frolicked in the autumn mist in a land called Honali
Huff the magic dragon lived by the sea
And frolicked in the autumn mist in a land called Honali"

"My uncle used to sing this song," Nac stated into his mic.

"Really?"

"Yeah, he was a great musician. Not famous or anything, but he was good. When I got older he said it was a song about smoking pot, but I still prefer to remember it as if I were a kid, just a child and his imaginary dragon friend."

"Hah, I've never heard this song before. It's catchy. I'll stick to Bob when I'm getting ripped."

"All Beatles for me."

"White people." Nac heard vines soft laughter in his ear.

Once the singer finished the song, the entire area clapped. Nac looked past the singer to the see night descending over the crowd and the marina. The darkness was broken by sporadic lamps placed around the white walking paths.

"That's it for me tonight, ladies and gentlemen. Please keep an eye on the water as the real show is about to begin." Greg placed his guitar into its case at the corner of the stage. All of the children left the stage and returned to their parents. Greg disappeared into the throng of tourists and families. People scattered, setting up picnic blankets in the grassy areas with direct sight over the water.

Nac took another bite of his ice cream and watched the Shaw family gather their belongings and move to an open area of grass. He followed and took up his sentinel post a hundred feet away. On the opposite side at the far edge of the picnic area he saw Vine standing, alertly watching anyone who approached the family.

The crowd gasped in unison. The sky lit up as a giant firework exploded over the harbor. Shimmering blue sparkles rained over the spectators. Moments later another loud crack rang through the air. Red shimmers fell chaotically from the explosion down into the harbor below. Explosion after explosion rang out. Every color imaginable rained down from the sky. Claps and cheers sounded out from all directions. Even the gnats seemed to be taking a break from biting as the spectacle continued.

The pace of the display seemed to increase. Barrage after barrage of color and sound exploded into the air. A loud crack pierced the cacophony of sound. A flash of blue appeared in the middle of the picnicking crowd.

"Shooter in the lighthouse!" Vine screamed into Nac's ear.

Nac dropped his ice cream. Sprinkles bounced off the ground. The spoon clattered out of the disposable bowl and landed on the white sandy path. He sprang forward, running to the attacker.

"I'm lasing the whole target. Get there," Nac heard as he sprinted down the pathway toward the lighthouse. He weaved through the crowd at a full run, dodging parents holding hands of small children. As he ran, the left side of his face illuminated periodically from the exploding fireworks over the water. Thick metal chains dangled between concrete pillars a foot off the ground on the left side of the path serving as a barrier to the dark harbor water below gently lapping against the concrete wall of the harbor itself. Green grass dotted with families lined the right side. Nac sprinted past a couple who separated for a moment to let him pass as he charged down the dark pathway.

He reached the end of the path alongside the harbor edge and turned toward the lighthouse at full speed. Small white stones kicked up into the air. Brown streaks appeared in the pathway as he left behind a mark to his haste. Sprinting up to the lighthouse he reached a small metal gate serving as the only barrier to entry and quickly hopped over the divider.

He reached the door and it slammed open with a bang. The lock appeared melted and completely useless. The door bounced off the interior wall and slammed back into the threshold as Nac entered the dark room. The unserviceable door swung back inward slightly, leaving almost a foot opening to the outside world. Light streamed in from the opening, barely illuminating the dark interior of the lighthouse.

He looked around the roughly twenty foot in diameter circular room. A metal staircase started at the back wall and ran up the inside to the right. It ascended circularly attached to the inner walls of the building. A few small display tables lined the rest of the wall on the ground floor displaying Hilton Head throughout time. The room was deathly still. Nac's fast paced breathing was the only sound, interrupted periodically by the sound of the pyrotechnics exploding over the nearby water.

He reached down and pulled his sidearm from his ankle holster hidden under his blue jeans pants leg. He chambered a round and keyed his mic. "I'm inside." He looked up to see the spiraling staircase disappear into the darkness above.

Movement.

He dropped to his knees and rolled to the right inside the circular room. A blue cocoon flashed around him.

He aimed at the dark space where he'd seen movement, his eyes barely able to see after the flash of his shield. Bullets pinged against the wall behind him, and he heard the whizz of steel passing his head. He fired into the darkness. A body fell from the stairs above, vanishingjust before impact with the concrete bottom. A metal machine gun clattered to the floor. Red trails of blood splashed across the concrete.

Nac reached into his left pocket and pulled out a large optical display. It fit over his face like large glasses. It calibrated for a moment, then went fully transparent.

"You ok?"

"Yeah."

"I'm still lighting up the tower. There's no way they can put out an accurate round. Let me know when you reach the top and I'll come to back you up," Vine's voice rang into Nac's ear.

"Roger."

He keyed a button on the visor near his left ear. The display changed to thermal readouts. A bright humanoid form was revealed near the top, quickly descending the stairs.

"One hostile and he's incoming. He's moving down the stairs now. I'm waiting at the bottom to ambush."

Nac toggled his headset again to a readout of electrical currents. The room was utterly dark with the exception of the human figure moving quickly down the stairs. His body was lined with a bright neon blue glow betraying the advanced weaponry he was utilizing. The lines of blue appeared to flow in various directions on his body, displaying the figures electrical circulatory system pumping power instead of blood.

Something resting on his right hip was a dense swirling mass of bright neon blue light. It stung Nac's eyes despite the default dampening maximum setting on the optics filter. The weapon in his hand shone brightly. The magazine handle was bright blue indicating specialized rounds.

"I'm en route," Vine sprinted toward the lighthouse.

Nac continued to scan the building as the figure descended the metal staircase. He noted a thin blue line about halfway up the stairs with no trail leading off to the rest of the building. The only other electrical readouts were attached to the quickly approaching figure. As the blue form reached the midpoint of the stairs, it froze and grew smaller.

Nac concealed himself beside a sturdy table displaying a replica of Harbor Town. The staircase went just barely over his head, giving him an ideal spot for ambush once the target reached the floor.

The figure finally stood, and continued its methodical descent. His heart raced with each step the approaching figure took. He modified his headset to normal vision and looked up. Unable to see much in the darkness, he waited for his eyes to adjust to the interior of the concrete structure. Loud footfalls echoed throughout the room, getting closer with each strike of boot heel on metal. Each strike seemed to insult Nac's being.

The foyer where Nac hid was dark. His vision was still compromised but improved every second. He looked up at the spiraling staircase. It disappeared into darkness after only thirty feet. In the darkness the top was invisible to the naked eye. The footfalls continued to get closer as whomever was coming quickly ran down, hitting each step in a staccato rhythm.

Finally, Nac saw a hand sliding down the railing on the lowest level of stairs across from him as the footfalls reached an even louder level. His heartbeat sounded like a bass drum in his head. His breathing slowed. He could hear Vine's heavy breathing in his ear as his partner charged down the white pathway outside. Nac adjusted his crouch at the side of the table and pointed his pistol at the base of the stairs. He realized the footfalls had stopped short.

He held his breath for a moment to listen. Silence. The crack of firework explosions rocked the outside world, but sounded muted inside the thick concrete structure. Nac looked around again and saw no movement in the darkness. He reached up and keyed his electric sensor view. He blinked momentarily at the brightness, then looked around quickly. Nothing. No signals in any direction.

"I'm almost there!" he heard Vine yell into his headset.

Nac looked up just in time to see a blue glowing figure leap over the railing of the stairs directly over his head. The neon blue currents grew brighter as the figure attacked. His right hand clasped a glowing blue device with the outline of a gun, pointed toward Nac. Its eyes were shielded by a visor. A bright blue line bisected the face from temple to temple, all the way to the bottom of the nose.

As the figure fell the short distance, its left hand reached down and slammed the bright blue point on his hip. The figure went dark for a split second before being engulfed in a massive ball that was so bright the blue appeared closer to the white of the sun. Nac staggered backwards in his crouched position and felt his back push against the wall.

For a moment everything was a blinding white light. Before his vision cleared his training kicked in, and he lurched forward. His shoulder made contact with a boot. He felt a knee impact his chin and body crumple over his head. He heard a groan and a loud thud of a heavy body hitting the floor. Bullets pinged against the concrete to his back. Metal gear components rattled against the concrete floor as the assailant recovered quickly. Bright spots dotted Nac's vision. He blinked rapidly trying to regain his sight.

He turned toward the noise and raised his weapon. He felt the recoil as the handgun went off silently in his hand. He heard loud cracks emanate through the room as bullets found the concrete of the wall. Nac's world exploded into pain as he was pushed backwards by a massive force to his right chest, another to his abdomen, and a third to his left lower ribs. His stagger was interrupted as hands grabbed his extended right arm still holding his sidearm. He felt his gun wrested from his grasp. As his vision finally cleared his world was turned upside-down. The man turned and dropped to a knee. Pulling Nac forward, he used Nac's momentum to throw him over his shoulder.

Nac landed flat on his back, head slamming into the concrete floor. As his head hit the ground he slid a few feet farther. A small blood stain lingered on the ground where his head landed. The man stood and drew another weapon, aiming at Nac's chest. Nac rolled sideways. The first two rounds pinged against the floor of the lighthouse. His roll stopped with a thud as his body connected with the very table which he'd been using to conceal himself before. His ribs exploded in pain as another round found his body armor. He grabbed his side and rolled onto his back, looking up to see the man aiming the weapon at his face. A sinister smile appeared behind the weapon.

Three quiet pops rang out in the dark concrete lighthouse.

The man lurched forward. Blood splattered across Nac's face. The man's head exploded outward. Stumbling forward for a second, the now lifeless body crumpled to the floor. The weapon fell harmlessly to the ground with a clang. Blood immediately began to pool underneath the man's destroyed head. The lifeless body twitched on the ground. Darkness took him.

Chapter 6

His eyes fluttered open. The center of his very being was only pain. A cough teased his ribs into announcing their presence, and turned to a wince. He attempted to sit up, breathed in, and kicked his ankles over the side of the bed. He groaned and grabbed his ribs in agony. Pain radiated outward from his entire core.

Leaning back he felt a sense of relief. Nac looked around at his current situation. White walls were everywhere. He looked down and saw plain white sterile sheets. An IV was sticking out of his left arm. He moved to pull it out. The pain in his head hit him like a truck. He let the cocktail continue, and rubbed his throbbing forehead with his right hand, feeling a thick bandage preventing skin on skin contact. He noticed that the bandage didn't cover the crown of his head, but that there was a very thick bandage over the back right side of his skull.

Alum rushed into the room with a smile. "I'm glad to see you're awake," she said, grabbing a clipboard from the door. Nac turned to look at her. Her white overcoat sat atop a shiny lavender blouse tucked neatly into solid white pants. “You have a pretty serious concussion and several bruised ribs, but overall you’re fine. A few days rest and you’ll be back on your feet."

“How’s Marcus?"

“Marcus is safe. He survived, thanks to your efforts.”

Nac sighed and closed his eyes. He leaned back and his eyes darted open. Her hand pulled back hastily. “I’ll send in your guests,” she stated flatly and quickly walked out of the room.

Nac turned his head to the side to look with a pained smile as Vine, Diana, and Griz bounced into the drab room. Vine came to his bed at the front of the group wearing a neon Lavender vest and shiny silver pants. Diana stepped out from behind Vine’s frame with a look of deep concern. Her blond hair flowed down past her shoulders. Her pale white shoulders were cut by thin straps of a light pink tank top resting on dark blue jeans and pink flats.

Griz brought up the rear in his Civil War look with his old blue heavily buttoned overcoat. He also wore a white button up shirt with a frilly collar, tucked into all black jeans and black calf high boots with a two inch sole. His normal thick visor was still attached to his face. Large brown spikes popped above his head seemingly at nearly six inches in length.

“You done napping?" Vine asked.

“What happened?”

“After you went full Air Force and took a nap on me, I hooked both of you up to my alternate bands and brought you back to HQ.”

“How long have I been out?”

“Just a few hours. Alum said you’ll be out of here tomorrow if all goes well."

"All of your gear was fried," Griz interjected. "I analyzed the equipment from the assailant, and it looks like he used an electromagnetic pulse on you. I've never seen a handheld EMP before. The power requirements are typically too great for someone to carry into combat. The hip capacitor may be the key. The technology is pretty amazing," he added. His voice increased in pitch slightly as he talked about the new technology. "I think this is how they've circumvented our protection protocols."

"Any idea who he was?"

"DNA readouts show it was an NP agent we call 'Jabak.' He's one of their low level enforcers, born into NP service by his parents. He's been NP muscle since he was fourteen," Diana answered. "He was trained to be an agent from birth."

"You're lucky," Griz added. "We've seen Jabak in action before. He's a complete sadist. There are stories of him in the aftermath of some battles from the first campaign. He'd babble on about how he's actually saving people, purifying them with pain, for the sin of fighting the prophecy. Each act he did to them, he at least said he thought it was for God. Rumor has it he travelled to the Spanish Inquisition just for shits and giggles."

"Lucky? I think I've learned my lesson. I need to get up to speed on all the tech before I go back out. I can't just rely on my looks anymore." Nac glanced at Diana.

"Modesty has always been your strength," Diana chided.

"You are lucky. Jabak must have pissed someone off. We rarely get outright wins like this. Stationery defenses, remember. Think of yourself more as bait, it helps," Vine added.

"How did you keep him from taking a second shot at Marcus?"

"I always carry a wall. It's a wide area laser. You ever fuck with a cat? It's like that, except you can scale it to hit an entire building. It's standard light infantry anti-sniper gear. Keep the enemy under control, advance, destroy. You performed perfectly, until you got your shit kicked," Vine grinned.

"Alum says you need one more day under her care minimum, but you have no serious injuries. After that you're free to go once you feel ready. Also, Dr. G. wants to give the senator a little motivation. He's going to take him to control. If you're back on your feet you might be able to join them."

"What's Control? You've mentioned it before."

"You'll find out soon enough. I don't know what it looks like anymore. It's been so long since I've been," Vine answered. "I'm looking forward to going back."

"Oh, I suggest you heal quickly. While you were out, Alum convinced Dr. G. to have a celebration. He's normally so somber and unyielding. I have no idea how Alum got him to agree to it, but it's in two days. No jumps at all for the day. We've never had something like this before," Griz added.

"I'll be there," Nac responded weakly, and closed his eyes for several seconds.

"For now, we need to get back to command," Diana stated. "We're still sending out the last two protection missions today. Not all of us get the day off."

"We were supposed to be there ten minutes ago, but when we heard that you were waking up we figured it was worth Dr. G's shit to wait. Besides, we're with Alum, so we're safe. She's the miracle worker," Vine added.

Griz and Vine quickly strode out while Diana lingered for a moment. She looked down, then raised her eyes to meet Nac's gaze. "I'm glad you're okay," she said so softly he could barely make out her words. She cleared her throat

"Me? Don't worry about me. I'm invincible," he replied with clear hubris. He saw deep concern and became lost for a moment. Her eyes conveyed a kind of warmth and caring. Her face bore an equal mark of concern and she stood, rocking side to side slightly on her small flats with her hands clasped behind her back.

"So, what's this I hear of Alum's hold over Dr. G. How do we learn her secrets?"

Diana laughed, snorting gently "Of course you joke. If only you knew. I've been here almost five years and we've never been able to let loose. Something's up."

"I mean, there's a whole day where nobody can jump. Where are you picturing me taking you first?"

She smiled, lowering her gaze to the large white bandages on his chest. "Ladies and vagabonds? That always ends well for the vagabond."

"Alps circa 1999 to ski? Carnival in Rio during American Dream? Watch Apollo 11 blast off for the moon? Here, now?"

She chewed her lip and smiled in silence. She cocked her head to the side and looked up. "Madagascar." The single world breathlessly escaped her lips in barely a whisper.

"What? Why Madagascar?"

"It has cute animals. Have you ever seen a baby sifaka? How about a pack of fossas? They're absolutely adorable."

"You're a cute animal."

She looked down, shaking her head, and bit her lip, arms reaching across her abomen, hands clasping at her own hips. A large smile broke out over her face. "I look forward to it." Her eyes sparkled as she replied.

Griz popped his head back inside the room, the large brown spikes made an appearance well before his head. "Diana, you coming?"

"Yes," she answered quickly. Pausing for a moment, she looked to Nac in his bed, then spun on her right foot to face the exit and quickly glided back outside. Nac watched her leave, noting how graceful she made even the slightest movement.

Alum walked back into the room carrying her clipboard with current medical readouts. She smiled coyly. "I'll set you up with a sling for when you leave if you need it. I'm guessing your right shoulder will be a little sore and some movement will cause pain. All in all, you should be fine. I think you'll be fully operational in a week. You don't need to stay here past tonight. Just try to rest whenever you can."

"Sounds good, Doc."

As Alum turned to leave, Nac stopped her. "Alum, one question." She turned to look at him quizzically. "What's Diana's story?"

"What do you mean?" She asked, stifling a smile. Her eyes sparkled.

"Well, where is she from? What does she do when she's not running things in the operations center? Help a guy out?"

"Why don't you ask her?" Alum answered and quickly walked back outside.

The next day in the clinic passed quickly for Nac as he entertained himself with a combination of the amazing painkillers and a few immersive movies streamed onto his visor. Early the next afternoon he finally got to exit the care of Alum and returned to his dorm room. He walked through the now familiar maze of hallways and finally reached his room. Walking inside, he lay on his bed, relaxing in the comfort of his space. He rolled to his left side and groaned in pain as his sore ribs contacted the stiff mattress. He reached over and grabbed his red rally towel. Clutching the bright red fabric, he drifted into a drug induced sleep.

He slept all night and most of the next day. A few hours into the next evening he rose and quickly dressed. He donned a sharp white button up dress shirt which he left untucked over straight leg dark blue jeans and sleek brown shoes. He rolled up the sleeves on his shirt and walked out to the main dining facility. People seemed to be coming from all directions, all heading toward the cavernous gathering place. Everyone was smiling. Boisterous chatter sprung from small groups of people. Nac found his place in the crowd and glanced around, laughing to himself at the sheer variety of people present.

Walking to his left was a man with light white skin. He appeared dressed in a mesh orange shirt with bright yellow suspenders hanging down to hold matching yellow pants. The pants ended just below his knees leaving his calves bare for a few inches. Calf high orange socks disappeared underneath bright orange shoes.

The man was walking with a woman in similar attire. She had tan skin and wore a sheer white top. It had a deep plunging neckline. The top ended several inches above her belly button. A bright pink bra was clearly visible underneath. Her pants seemed to be in two parts. The top part consisted of a white waistline with bold pink belt buckle. The white shorts were very short and incredibly tight. At the bottom of the boyshorts her skin was exposed for several inches until matching white stripes appeared above and below the knees in one inch thick straps. She also wore matching white sandals with straps crisscrossing up her ankles all the way to the strap below her knees.

Looking to the right was a couple dressed much more similarly to Nac's time. The man wore a sharply tailored blue shirt and grey pants with a bright solid red tie. The woman holding his hand was wearing a sharp black cocktail dress and walked delicately in matching black four inch high heeled stilletos. She clasped her date's right arm with both hands as she moved with the crowd.

Nac rounded the corner and fell into place behind the two more colorfully dressed individuals and proceeded into the dining facility. As he entered, he paused for a moment. A greeter welcomed him to the party and handed him a drink. The couple bumped into him from behind, forcing him forward. He slid out of the moving crowd and stared open-mouthed at the scene before him.

The massive dining hall was nearly full, and more people continued to pour in. There were at least a thousand people present. The tables and chairs had all been cleared out aside from a few dozen tables to the back right of the main room. Nac looked to the large display on the side of the hall; 19:58. He took a drink from his neon yellow cup and grimaced. The alcohol was incredibly strong, reminding him of Augustan moonshine. He took another sip and the burn faded.

He weaved his way through the densely packed crowd looking for a familiar face until he noted some brown spikes poking up above the crowd. He made his way in that direction and walked up to join Griz standing near the center of the room. Griz's face was devoid of his normal visor, revealing his full babyface. He wore a white long sleeve shirt with shiny silver buttons, maroon pants with several half inch thick cords dangling from random places, and thick black calf high boots with his usual two inch thick sole.

To his right stood the girl Nac remembered seeing when he first arrived at the facility working with Diana. She wore knee high black boots with a hefty black sole. Fishnet stockings rose from the boots to end under a victorian black skirt. The flow of the skirt was cut by a stringent dark purple corset which curved inward sharply and rose to above her chest. She also wore frilly black fingerless gloves and a tight black choker. Her short brown hair was pulled back under an equally frilly black hat. From her left ear, an opaque plastic panel blocked her face so that only her red lips and pinkish white chin appeared below the dark screen. Her head jerked to the side intermittently, matched by occasional full body spasms.

"Griz! What's the word?"

"Hey, How are you feeling?"

"I'll be good as new in no time," he answered.

"Good. I don't think you've met my sister, Arwen." He punched the girl, causing her to yelp and key her headset.

"I told you not to interrupt me when I'm gaming." She scolded her brother, then her eyes went wide as she spotted Nac. She stepped behind her larger brother, running her left hand down her skirt while her right hand ran through her hair.

Nac reached out his hand and smiled, waiting a moment as she stepped forward to clasp his hand. The fabric covering her skin scraped across his bare skin.

"It's nice to meet you."

"Likewise," she replied with little interest and turned back to the main room. Her head drooped, and she stole a glance back to Nac, then keyed her visor back to opaque. Her body immediately became more rigid.

"Where's everyone else?"

"Diana is with Dr. G. for the announcement to start the festivities. I haven't seen Vine around, but I'm sure he's here. He can't be too hard to find. Hey, I have a question for you."

"Shoot."

"So, there's this--" His voice trailed off as Dr. G. stepped into view, climbing atop a makeshift stage in the middle of the hall that must have been built overnight. He wore nearly his standard attire, white button up short sleeve silk shirt, light powder blue shorts, and sandals. He reached down and helped Diana up to the stage.

Nac felt the world slow down as he looked up at her. She wore a form-fitting bright green dress with a slender neckline plunging several inches below her collarbone. The dress was flawless, interrupted only by a vibrant tropical pink-colored belt about half an inch wide. Long vibrant red hair flowed down from her head. Lost for a moment, he didn't even notice as a hush fell over the group. Dr. G. started to address the crowd. After a few moments he snapped back to reality and focused on Dr. G's booming voice.

"--going smoothly so far. If everything continues as planned, we should have a readout on the campaign in a few weeks. Thank you all for your help. Your dedication and hard work are what make this possible, are what create hope, are what gives the future of humanity a fighting chance. Every breath you take, every day you live fully, is proof that we will not go quietly and that life is worth fighting for." He paused for a moment as the crowd cheered loudly. The roars rose and fell, single voices intertwined in a joyous uproar of approval. It slowly died down as Dr. G. held his hand up to request silence.

"The campaigns have been taxing. We have all given much. We have all lost much. But," he paused and his voice rose to a thunderous pitch "We have also won much! Look what a few vestiges can do." The crowd roared, enabling the older man to take a breath.

"Four hundred years, and hundreds of billions of lives are possible because of your efforts." The raucous crowd cheered loudly for nearly thirty seconds until Dr. G. raised his hand to quiet the mob.

"Enough with the formalities," he boomed. "We're here to celebrate. Celebrate life. Celebrate hope. Forget your worries. Forget the past. Forget the future. Get fucked!" As he finished he pumped his yellow cup high into the air. A small wave of liquid rolled over the top of the glass and onto the stage below. The crowd cheered and he took a swig of his drink. Everyone present with a drink roared an animalistic cry, and followed through. Dr. G. turned to the back of the stage and gave a thumbs up signal. Loud electronic bass rang out in the cavernous room, bouncing off the walls.

Dr. G. stepped down from the platform as the entire company began to dance. Bodies moved together with the music blaring above. Nac moved off to the side as Griz began to jump and slide across the dance floor. Nac weaved his way back to the edge of the crowd, sipping the caustic drink in his hand. He worked his way toward the stage along the border of the crowd. Sweat from the dancers filled the air, mixing with a different scent.

As he moved across the room, he saw a large group of people sitting at a circular table around a giant device. Above it hung a sign that read 'Battle of the Ironclads.' Underneath it read 'Innovation creates Obsolescence." A third line read "Obsolescence creates Desperation." The entire beast was a cylinder, ten feet in diameter. The base was black metal extending two feet high. Atop the wrought iron base, a foot of clear water lapped gently against the glass, followed by six feet of open air.

Two women, barefoot, wearing tiny daisy dukes and crop tops emblazoned with the word "Merrimac", pumped large bellows at either side of the base. They pumped in unison, and everyone in the circle slapped the ground with each burst of air into the device.

A suspendered but shirtless man with a massive grey beard and corn cob pipe stood at the base of the beast in weathered jean shorts. Florida Man. He held a torch over his head in a display of caveman barbarice, then smiled to the circle. He turned to the beastly device, and slid the metal grate to the side. He kicked three, six inch sided, dark green spheres into the newly exposed opening. At least fifty more were stacked neatly nearby. The man threw the torch into the grate.

"Merrimac," the drumming men boomed.

"Ambrosia," the drumming women answered.

The Merrimac girls pumped faster. The water bubbled. The top chamber swirled with clouds. Hands slapped the table and boots struck ground. Booms echod behind him in the distance. The smoke solidified into a dense mass. The women stood and kicked the bellows to the side. One reached down and grabbed a massive mallet at her feet, while the other rolled a drum into view. She swung the hammer, it connected with a boom, and everyone present slapped the table. The top of the device unfurled with over fifty hoses snaking down. Nac heard the boom echo in the distance.

"Merrimac," the drumming men boomed.

"Ambrosia," the drumming women answered.

A hundred hands drumrolled as the Merrimac girls organized the hoses. The man grabbed a cube in each hand, raising them above his head. He dropped the first one, and nimbly kicked it inside the monster with only a single touch.

"Merrimac," everyone boomed.

The man dropped the second cube. As it touched his foot, hands hit the floor. He hacked. Hands boomed in time. Five touches, in perfect control. His showboating ended with a no look back heel.

"Ambrosia," everyone boomed, and rose. Grabbing a hose, the base of the interior chamber glowed a neon green. A light show in the smoke began.

Smoke billowed in all directions as everyone took huge pulls from the device and blew smoke into the air. Nac noticed the air shimmered in a perfect cube surrounding the gathering, with the device at the very center. He smiled and grabbed a hose. A few members chanted with each puff, steadily decreasing in intensity.

He felt a tap on his shoulder.

"I thought I'd find you here." And there she was. A smile betraying no coyness appeared on his face.

She remained stoic, turned and grabbed a hose. She whipped around. Her vibrant red hair spun with her as she moved nearly hitting him in the chin. She slapped the tip of his hose with her own, and took a drag without pause. She smiled as she exhaled.

"The Monitor girls are hotter."

"What's that?"

"The competition." She immediately took another drag. She looked up and smiled as she inhaled as long as possible, removing her lips to exhale.

She looked up at him in silence as he smoked. As he exhaled, he grabbed her hand. "Come with me. I want to show you something."

She hesitated, taking one last drag, cocking her head to the side skeptically, then dropped the hose. He pulled her through the smoke barrier and into the ravenous crowd. He looked back to watch her gracefully move. She smiled shyly as they jostled through the crowd. The dance reached a new crescendo. The bass rang out as electronic music overpowered all other noise except for the low roar of the crowd as it moved.

The room was raucous. Dancers leapt high into the air. People gyrated to the beat. Couples ground together in unison. The crowd moved in a mass of compressed flesh. Neon cups littered the floor, wet with a mix of sweat and spilled drinks. Smoke billowed from several different stations to fill the room. The ceiling itself seemed to have a foot thick layer of dense smoke condensed at the top.

Reaching the exit to the room Nac looked back over his shoulder. He looked past the increasingly energetic crowd and saw a smiling Alum wrap her arm around Dr. G. and point towards him. Great, Nac thought to himself, I'm sure I'll get chewed out about this somehow. As he turned back to lead Diana he missed Dr. G. break out into a toothy smile, and pull Alum against his body.

The duo moved down the hallway away from the celebration. Couples, hand in hand, ran past toward the dormitory. Latecomers to the party ran by in the opposite direction to catch up to the festivities.

The sounds of the celebration slowly faded into the distance until finally the two rounded a corner to peace and quiet. Nac led the way as Diana hurried after him. The sound of her footsteps rang out in the confined corridor as her fiery red heels tapped against the drab concrete floor. Nac finally came to a stop near the middle of a long hallway. Diana looked at him, with a skeptical face. He reached out and took her left hand. "Ready?"

She nodded in reply. He pushed the door open and they stepped inside. It took Nac a moment for his eyes to adjust to the brightness. Before him was a spectacular green grassy area with large green trees scattered about. Flowers were neatly planted in long beautiful colors. To the right a tree was surrounded by a ring of white and pink roses. To the left, another tree rose from a field of purple irises with bright yellow centers. Several moss-covered benches dotted the open area. The air smelled fresh, unlike anywhere else in the compound.

Before Nac could take it all in, Diana kicked off her shoes. She ran barefoot across the soft grass toward a small path. Nac followed closely behind, jogging to keep up.

The path continued for about a hundred feet, surrounded on each side by perfectly spaced trees creating a tunnel of strong tree limbs and vibrant green leaves. The path ended abruptly, spilling the pair out into small grassy opening. Trees lined the sides of the small pasture. A tiny pond sat in the middle. Bright orange fish could be seen swimming in the shallow waters. The shoreline was lined with orchids of every color. Clusters of purple, red, white, green, and yellow all combined together to surround the glistening pond. The sweet scent of the flowers filled the air. The only sound Nac could hear was the soft rippling of the pond's waves lapping against the floral edge.

Diana paused for a moment at the exit of the tunnel of trees. She looked out over the beautiful clearing, then rushed forward to the pond. As she approached, she twirled once, her dress rising as she spun. She sighed contentedly and sat down on the grass, breathing deeply through her nose to enjoy the smell of the field of flowers. Their pungent aroma permeated the air like sweet honey.

"I wanted to show you this place. I thought you might like it."

"Really? You wanted to show me this spot?

"Yeah."

"You know I made this, right?"

"No, I didn't, but I think that clearly shows that my instincts are right.

"You're." She stopped and shook her head. "So dumb."

"This is my favorite place," she said. "I come here almost every day to relax and remember what life used to be like." She lay back into the grass and rolled over onto her stomach, kicking her feet in the air and wiggling her toes.

Nac looked around at the scenery, then back to Diana now laying on her back in the grass. Her chest rose and fell with each breath. A smile of pure contentment adorned her face. "What life used to be like, huh? What's your story?"

She sat up and looked to the water. "I've lived all over, but California mainly. It's warm. There are mountains on one side and ocean on the other. It's not cold."

"I got it, you get the thermostat. How'd you end up

here?"

"I was an engineer. I was working on an adaptation to the personal environmental controls so that they could cover homes, buildings, and eventually entire cities. One day, NPs did what NPs do."

Diana waited a moment, recognizing his silence as an invitation. "I loved to cook when I was younger. I could have been a chef, but I always loved numbers. They made sense to me. That's what got me started on the path to engineering. But I'm more than just a nerd. My dad was a huge outdoorsman, and the area around Los Angeles had everything. He taught me to surf when I was young. We used to go together every Saturday morning. He taught me to love nature, and respect it, and to hate filthy hippies who shit on the beach."

She paused with a smile.

"Not that I've ever witnessed that, multiple times. So, that's why I insisted Dr. G. put this area in the compound. There are two of them, on alternating daylight cycles. Any time we want we can come into one of the rooms and get the feeling of a beautiful California day. This pond is actually my favorite. Orchids are my favorite flower. I can sit here all day, smell them, and watch the fish swim."

"What about you? What was Will's childhood like before all of this?" she asked mischievously.

"Haha, already checking up on me, are you?" She shook her head with a smile. "Well, I grew up in rural Virginia. My neighbor was my age and we used to just run around in the woods all day. It was pretty awesome. Then I had to become an adult."

"We can't all be Peter Pan. Honestly, I'm jealous. We were outdoors a lot, but we always had to have our PECs because ofthe heat."

"What's the meaning of 'Diana'? Another princess?"

"No." She mocked with evident chagrin. "She was my favorite goddess. Diana of the wildland, protector of the animals. Kind of a badass."

"Would you prefer to save the animals more than the humans?"

"Maybe," She replied with a smile. She looked up at him and brushed her hair out of her eyes. "I'm a huge fan of all animals. They're just so cute. Have you ever seen a baby sloth? Absolutely adorable. And, animals aren't as fucked up as people."

"Did you not have the discovery channel?"

"Ok, if they aren't trying to eat you, most animals are cool."

Will reached his left hand behind her back and took her hand. She looked down for a moment, then up to meet his gaze. He reached up with his other hand and gently tilted her chin up as he leaned in. Eventually, he pulled back. He tilted his head forward so his forehead gently rubbed against hers. His eyes slowly opened to the sight of her beaming face, eyes bright.

"I have a secret I want to tell you," she said, and leaned forward into his ear. He reached his left arm around her and pulled her tight. Her soft chest pressed against his ribs, her mouth hovered near his left ear. Her breath felt warm against his skin. His spine tickled the base of his skull.

"Wait, is that?"

Her eyes sparkled slightly. She looked at him, paused momentarily, and nodded.

Chapter 7

The next several days passed quickly for everyone in the compound. The entire place was buzzing with lingering energy from the party. Life had been restored. Everyone had renewed focus and determination. Nac bore a giant shit-eating grin plastered across his face at all times. His steps felt a little lighter. His days seemed happier. He found himself focusing a little less, but it was allowed as he worked through his recovery. Even his sore ribs didn't dampen his spirits.

On the third day after the party Nac woke to find the bruising nearly gone. He went through his usual morning routine of six sun salutations. He finished his final lunge, stretching his hands high above his head in the self-named old man stretch, and stood near his bedside.

He noted the pain in his ribs and body was less, almost unnoticeable. He quickly dressed himself in his usual attire, simple white t-shirt with jeans and brown slip-on shoes. A few people had even started calling him Slips. Navigating the hallways no longer felt like a dull labyrinth scattered with unfamiliar faces. Instead, it was beginning to feel like home.

He strode through the halls and quickly reached the dining facility. He stepped inside and paused for a moment, as always, to take in the scene before him. The tables had been restored to their locations prior to the party. The Ironclads had been removed. The room was full of bright faces as the residents began their days. Even in this place, humanity found a routine that worked.

Nac wove his way through the seating area and headed to the back of the room where a small line awaited their turn to order food. No matter what time of day, there was always food available, and there was always a line of people waiting to eat. He found his place in line and waited.

He grabbed the main course of the morning, G's biscuits and gravy. He snagged an apple and some carrots with hummus to finish off the meal, then moved to the refrigerators. He grabbed a few cartons of milk then a glass mason jar with a brownish liquid inside. The holographic label showed a man in overalls sitting on a front porch with a modest wooden home at his back. He endlessly rocked back and forth in a weathered brown wooden rocking chair with a piece of grass poking out of his mouth. Above the man in the hologram the label read Sweetness. To the bottom was the phrase 'A sweet drink for the sweet life.'

Nac quickly walked off to the dining area. Not seeing anyone he knew, he grabbed a seat at an empty table. The one thing missing from his new morning routine was a paper. There was no daily publication of the events that had transpired in the world. There was no phone to check for daily updates. Between bites of his meal, he glanced at the people around him. Some tables clearly revealed the formulation of cliques while others seemed completely random.

To the left was a table with a group of women dressed for the Kentucky Derby. They all were wearing vibrant patterned dresses and large summer hats. They chatted amongst themselves with occasional bursts of laughter.

The table behind them captured his attention completely. A group of augeys dominated two tables. Nearly ten in all. One of the women had embedded black irises that emitted a faint glow. Her blinks quickly became a nuisance.

A couple sat behind the woman with the glow in the dark eyes. Both the man and woman were dressed plainly in mostly dark colors. Their jeans looked heavily worn and naturally aged. Nac noticed each had eyes of unblemished pure white. Their irises were replaced with black lightning bolts diagonally striking downwards, toward the nose. The bolt thickness changed by roughly twenty micrometers as they chatted. Their lips were a matching blackish burgundy, never parting, and only emitting a faint indistinguishable white noise as each took their turn.

Each turned, in total silence, stood and walked quickly from the table. The rest of the group jumped up to follow. Glow in the dark girl approached Nac with a condescending smirk.

"They're attuned. You wouldn't understand. I bet you never even got a tattoo." She pivoted on her heel without waiting for a reply, and briskly strode after the pack.

Nac leaned back in his chair, picking up the mason jar. Should've just gotten a promise ring, dude, he thought with a shake of his head, and took a sip of the drink from the jar. A smile immediately formed as he realized the drink was actually the perfect nectar of the gods, sweet tea. He looked at the labeling of the man in the rocking chair and took another drink. It was perfect. There's almost no such thing as too sweet tea, but this was about perfection in a bottle.

He looked to his right. The table closest appeared to be a smattering of people from different eras. One man was of light complexion and dressed in a steampunk fashion similar to Griz and Arwen. He had a long well groomed dark brown beard which extended at least ten inches from his chin and a matching mustache. The tips of his mustache were curled to point up toward the brim of his hat, a six inch high navy blue top hat with black brim.

He also had on a matching navy blue tuxedo with no tails. A dark red vest was underneath the coat with ten gold buttons in two lines of five from top to bottom. Popping above the vest was a white dress shirt with a thick black tie clearly tied in a double windsor knot. Technology was spread throughout his appearance, ranging from the round glasses with text and images intermittently appearing to a large bulky wristwatch. Nac guessed the man must have been from the twenty-fifth century.

That first man was talking with another man to his right at the small round table of five. The companion had on bright neon colors as though Andre Agassi of the 1990s were his stylist. He appeared Asian, and his shirt, if you can call it that, was a mix of shiny silver and black in an intricate pattern that could be confused as a rorschach test. The shoulders were bright red with a strip of red forming a V reaching to about mid-sternum. His pants were a matching solid red while his shoes bore the same black and silver shine. Probably a post-industrial twenty-third century vestige.

Another man sat to the right, listening intently. He was dressed in the lavender fashion from the late twenty-first century. His shirt was a fairly standard white polo in contrast to his dark skin while his pants alternated in vertical stripes of lavender. He ended his dual look, part wild pattern, part conservative, with sharp black shoes and a lavender buckle over the tongue.

Engrossed in their own conversation were two women at the table. The one closest to the lavender man had pale white skin and must have also been from the same time as she wore a lavender dress which spiraled from above and below her waist, converging on a single point directly above her belly button. She completed her outfit with neon lavender wedge heels. She laughed excitedly as she listened to her companion who was much more conservatively dressed. She had on a standard business outfit which betrayed no time of origin. It was a simple dark navy blue pant suit and black flats. She had dark black skin and hair, pulled back by a matching dark navy blue headband.

Nac took another sip of his drink and wondered about each of their stories. He debated joining them to ask, but he both knew the rules and realised he only had five minutes to be in the command center. Today he would visit Control for the first time. Today, he would learn what Control meant.

He leaned back in his chair, taking another sip from the mason jar in his hand, and marveled for a moment. All of these people, each a memory of their time, united through unknown circumstances, to work in harmony for a common goal. He became filled with a sense hope.

He finished his delicious sweet tea and stood, collecting all of his garbage. He walked over to the receptacles, disposed of his trash, and briskly walked toward the command center. He weaved through the hallway, dodging a few other members of The Bulwark, and reached the main operating center. He walked in to see Vine already there with Marcus. Both men were dressed in dark dress pants and white shirts. They stood at one of workstations listening intently to Diana. She had her back to Nac, but he could see she wore form-fitting light blue long pants and white blouse. Nac couldn't help but take in her curves while she wasn't looking. Her long red hair cascaded down her back as she continued her briefing.

Nac began to walk over to join the group and saw Griz and Dr. G. nearby also listening intently. Dr. G. was dressed in his usual white short sleeve silk shirt, shorts, and sandals. He appeared nervous, biting the nail on his right thumb as he listened to Diana.

Griz was as outrageous as ever. He was wearing a dark brown leather vest with a golden yellow scarf wrapped around his neck. A large black shoulder pad sat on his right shoulder with a leather strap and several burnished gold buckles keeping it affixed. The strap swung down from the shoulder pad and ended under his left ribs. Appearing beneath the vest was a bright yellow long sleeve shirt. His pants were a dark black and navy blue camouflage pattern ending just below the knees to his usual black boots with large soles. His brown spikes were contained beneath a simple brown fedora, and his customary visor was over his eyes with a mirrored finish.

Hearing him approach, Diana turned around and paused. Her eyes brightened as she saw him but her face remained stoic. Nac somehow kept walking after momentarily almost tripping himself. He thought back to the past few days. He missed the warmth of her body pressed against his own, and her skills at chess. "Did I miss anything?" he asked.

"Yeah. We're getting Marcus here hooked up for his trip to Control. You'll be needing a PEC as well, Nac," Griz answered. "You'll need to be extra careful and prepare for an instant exit. We have no idea what the conditions will be."

"Okay. What do I need to do to prepare?"

Griz rummaged through the operations table and produced several small squares. Each was approximately four by four by one inch. "Attach these to your belts. Don't activate them until just before you jump. They'll provide both temperature control as well as protection from any harmful chemicals and radiation as long as it isn't too extreme. Do not jump without them turned on." He handed a cubic device with a belt clip and a transport wristband to Marcus, Dr. G., Vine, and Nac.

As Griz handed the last PEC to Nac, Dr. G interrupted. "Nac is staying here. Put that PEC away."

"What? You can't be serious."

"This trip is to orient Marcus, and Alum told me your concussion isn't fully healed yet. No jumps for a few more days. Next time." Dr. G. commanded. Nac stared into Dr. G.'s left eye for a moment, and saw zero give. He finally sighed in resignation.

The other three men quickly secured the wristband and the PEC device. Marcus hesitated before following the actions of Vine. They then headed up the steps to the jump platform. Turning around to face back toward Griz they each activated the PECs on their waists. The devices hissed quietly for several seconds until a small shimmer of dense air, barely visible to the naked eye, appeared in a bubble around each man. Griz raised his hand.

3,

2,

1,

He pressed the console, and the three men vanished. Nac turned to Diana and walked over to join her near the jump console. He slid his right hand into her left, and then gently pulled her hand back to her lower back. He pulled her against his body and she looked up as he leaned in for a kiss.

"I guess it's not all bad being stuck here." He smiled, and turned back to face the jump platform, knowing the trio would return shortly. As he turned back he saw Alum look away quickly, hiding her spying eyes from the couple. Diana leaned against Nac's ribs and his hand relinquished hers to find a better purchase on her hip.

Diana lifted up to her tiptoes and whispered in his ear, "I missed waking up in your arms th" She abruptly ended her statement as the three men reappeared on the jump platform. Marcus was already on his knees. He looked up and paused for a moment, face a pale green color, then twisted his head downward and retched onto the platform with a loud splash.

Vine leaned down and helped the Senator to his feet. "We really should think about tiling this floor. Something. Ever since we let Nac hang around, It's just gotten unsanitary. Anybody got any scotch guard?"

"Knock it off." Dr. G. harshly interrupted, then he looked to the ceiling. He closed his eyes and murmured to himself, then opened his eyes and stepped to the edge of the platform.

Alum walked up the two steps. She scanned each man

quickly as they passed. Dr. G. and Vine seemed unphased, while she noted the elevated heart rate and stress levels for Marcus.

"So that's why you call it Control?" Marcus asked, reaching the bottom step behind the other two men. "It's a way for you to measure your results like in a science experiment, isn't it?"

Dr. G. paused and looked back to the Senator. His eyes conveyed a sense of sadness, a sense of helplessness. Nac cocked his head in surprise. Something had shaken the unyielding. "Yes. Sometimes it gets better. Sometimes it gets worse. This time was discouraging." He ran his hand through his hair, and his eye focused. "I've seen worse."

He handed his computer readout to Diana, his hands visibly shaking. She removed a small data stick from the device and placed it in a slot on the computer. An amber light turned on. The computer immediately began to process the data, and after only a few moments several graphs popped up on the screen. Everyone huddled around as Diana began to explain the readings.

"The first graph is global human population levels." She indicated an erratic looking plot. She traced along to the first major blip where about twenty-five percent of the population decreased. "Here you can see the Saharan Bloodbath which occurred from 2139-2156.

"See that blip in 2142? That was me." Vine nudged Nac.

"It increased," Nac whispered.

"Exactly," he grinned.

"Wasn't that the week before I brought your crying, crayon eating ass here?" Dr. G retorted.

Diana interrupted the men. "If you can focus, the large vertical decline in 2156 was the nukings of several global capitals by the NPs. That was to be expected. As is the next two hundred and fifty years.

"Here is the biggest downturn yet." She indicated a vertical drop where population levels went from thirty-five billion to under one million between 2537 and 2538. "Data uploads stopped in 2538. The last readout shows some pretty startling information. Apparently the Russian government was looking to take some elite members of the country to a remote space station orbiting the moon."

"Why the moon?" Marcus asked.

"It looks like there was too much space junk in the areas closest to Earth. If you notice the one billion person population decrease in 2521, it says a Chinese space station in an orbit around Earth was destroyed by space particles. Keep in mind, we're talking about small pieces of steel moving thousands of miles an hour. The force of an impact at those speeds is tremendous. Just a small hole from a hit at the wrong spot can take out an entire facility when it's as precariously placed as a floating metal box in the vacuum of space. China blamed the Russians. The Russians cried innocent. As a result, a small fight between China and Russia broke out. It didn't go nuclear."

Marcus looked up in surprise. "One billion killed is a small skirmish?"

"Compare that to thirty-five billion lives lost only a few years later, and yes, it's pretty small," she snapped. "Let's move on. The Russians were apparently looking to abandon Earth. They had stockpiled fuel and other resources for the previous hundred years in a last-ditch effort to get a self-sustaining space station near the moon called 'Yekaterin-grad' named after Catherine the

Great. The station was already built, but hadn't been supplied. It was only housing a few cosmonauts at the time.

"It looks like the plan was to launch three ships full of citizens into space to populate Yekateringrad. Apparently the Americas were a part of the effort and had one ship. The Eurozone combined to populate the third ship. All three were planned for launch on September 23rd, 2537. There was a global outcry from those people and countries who felt they were being left behind.

"The NPs took advantage and destroyed all three ships on takeoff. The expected triumphant departure was broadcast live to the world, but became only a show of failure. All of the chosen destined for safety were killed. Among the dead were many political, economic, and social elites. It included the Queen of England, the President of the United States, and the Prime Ministers of Russia and Canada, the Venezuelan Premier, among others. Leaderless, they retaliated against the Chinese, Iranians, Japanese."

"Who the fuck nuked Canada?" Nac asked.

"Which time?"

"Gentlemen," Diana coughed. "It sparked full scale global nuclear war with no one left untouched. Even remote islands were destroyed."

Dr. G. looked around, seeing the horror on everyone's face. He heard the pain in Diana's voice as she fought to maintain her professionalism and continue the brief. Her voice cracked slightly as she talked of the death toll. "How did this happen? What happened to our efforts? How did Earth get to the point it needed to be abandoned?" he interrupted, giving her a break.

"One second, let me scan through." She paused, taking a deep breath. Everyone waited in silence, but each face revealed the strain of the information being received. “It looks like in the year 2072 a tech company based in Manhattan, New York called Terra Futures created a platform for futures trading which included trading for ‘the human fund.’

Its founders were Wall Street veterans. It created a way for people to profit on the fund decreasing in value." Anger cracked through her normally gentle voice. “They created a means of profit, an economic incentive, for the degradation of Earth. They took our plan and destroyed it. It doesn’t even look like NPs were involved. It was just natural."

“Let’s take a break for a minute,” Dr. G. interrupted again. “Arwen.” He waited as she hurried over from the back corner. She ran up wearing a white corset with black puffy shirt spilling out from underneath. She matched it with an ankle length black skirt and black thick heeled shoes disappearing under the long skirt. Her brown hair was pulled back into a long ponytail. Her monocle sat over her left eye devoid of any information readouts.

“Grab us all some drinks from the dining facility. Get some snacks, too." She nodded and hurried out the back of the room.

Diana returned to analyzing the data on the screens while the rest of the group sat down in the chairs surrounding the workstation. Everyone sat in silence as they let the information sink in. Marcus rubbed the top of his head in frustration. He slumped forward in his chair while staring at the floor. His eyes were wide with fear. His mouth was slightly open. He looked up and almost began to speak, then lowered his face and remained silent.

Arwen ran back in, heels tapping on the hard concrete

floor. She carried a tray of cheeses, crackers, and several assorted drinks. She placed it down on the workstation and scurried off to the back of the room. The group left the food untouched for a moment until Vine leaned forward and grabbed a hunk of cheese and a drink. He devoured the cheese in one bite, and snagged another. After a few moments, everyone finally reached in to take a piece. Most only nibbled.

Diana broke the silence. "It gets more disturbing."

She increased the size of a new graph. Initially the plotted value rose greatly, then fell all the way to near zero. "This is the graph of the value of the human fund." She pointed to the peak. "This is 2073. It took a year for the full implications of the futures trading to take over." She slid her hand along the graph showing the gradual decline until it reached a sharp drop of over twenty percent loss in a single year in 2095.

"Here, a multinational conglomerate from Russia, China, the US, and several other countries took massive short positions on the fund. Shortly after purchase they all deliberately increased emissions of greenhouse gases. The Chinese conglomerate even purchased a sewage company and began dumping directly into the Yangtze River. The fund value plummeted, and the companies made a huge profit.

"The trend continues downward at an increased rate until the end. Even in the last days, as the mission to reach Yekateringrad failed, others were deliberately destroying the world to make a profit. Shorting the stock netted a nearly twelve percent return for a three hundred year period. It was the safest high performance investment available.

"That's not all." She paused, her voice cracking again.

"Even the IMF custodians were taking advantage of the fund. The ten percent of all investments were still being diverted to them. However, since the IMF wasn't making any payouts as the fund decreased in value, they simply kept the money and funneled it back into global banking channels."

"Fucking bureaucrats." Marcus interrupted. "I deal with those people every day in Washington. Every time I think I've seen it all, they always find a way to surprise me."

The room went silent as everyone looked up to Diana, standing looking downcast in front of the team. After what seemed like an eternity, Dr. G. broke the somber mood. He stood and walked over to Diana, indicating the initial upward trend on the graph. "I think we can take this as encouragement. The fund was clearly working as intended. It rose over four hundred percent in the first fifty years of existence. All we have to do is prevent the futures trading and short selling of the stock."

Marcus shook his head in frustration and immediately countered. "I worked on Wall Street for years. It'll be a nearly impossible sell. Wall Street sees short selling as an essential component to how markets work. It's viewed as the flip side of the coin."

"We don't have to stop all short selling transactions," Alum added. "We just need to make the human fund into an equity that can't be traded in that manner. Make a one fund exception. Given the nature of the fund, it's easy to make the case. Blame it on the IMF if you have to. They're backing the fund after all. It's the only mutual fund in history to have that kind of support. I think it's quite reasonable."

"Marcus, we'll need you to be the lead on this. You

have time. You have a solid fifty-plus years to ensure it doesn't happen."

The senator stood, pushing his body upright with his hands on his thighs. He stood silently for a moment, looking at each person present, pausing for several seconds and locking eyes with each member of the team. Griz, Alum, Diana, Dr. G, Vine, and Nac all waited, watching him intently. He planted his feet and squared his shoulders toward Dr. G. "I'll get it done," he declared. The fear and shock in his eyes was replaced with stone cold resolve. "What choice do I have?"

Chapter 8

The next few days passed uneventfully for Nac. He spent most of his time in the armory with Grom going through weaponry. On the third day, as he hit the range trying out the grenade launcher configurations for the assorted rifles, Griz came charging in.

“I’ve figured it out!" he whooped to Nac, who remained in a prone position looking out over the range. He fired his last grenade round toggled to electrical detonation. It soared forward toward a cluster of virtual targets. He keyed the drone feature and directed the projectile to turn left. It landed in the middle of the grouping of targets and detonated. A thin blue wave emanated outwards and cut the virtual targets in half. Red holographic sparkles exploded outward from the virtual targets as they were shredded.

Nac smiled and rolled over, sitting up to face Griz. Upon first glance Nac noticed that he wasn’t wearing his visor. He looked tired. His normal babyface had dark circles under his eyes as though he hadn’t slept for days. Small fuzz appeared under his chin and above his mouth.

His white shirt had the sleeves rolled up to his elbows. His dark green vest bore dark smears and his hands had matching dark black stains across the fingers and palms. His dark navy blue pants looked equally unkempt, while his normal large soled black boots were marred with several fresh scuff marks. A dirty towel hung down from his pants seat pocket.

"What was that?"

"I figured it out!"

Grom walked over from the control center of the firing range. He wore his normal dark black pants tied into combat boots and black short sleeve shirt. His massive arms strained the fabric of the shirt. "Nice shot, Nac," He interrupted, pulling the weathered unlit cigar from his mouth. "You're getting the hang of drone nav."

Nac looked to Grom walking toward him, towering over Griz. "Now that I'm familiar with which button does what, I can direct it from my firing position. It's a pretty incredible tool. You said I can only give minor adjustments, right?"

"Correct. Use it to help you be more accurate. There's still no substitute for being a good shot." He paused for a moment, then looked to Griz, who had backed up to create space between himself and the much larger man. "Griz, what're you babbling on about?"

"The capacitor Jabak was using. I figured out how it works. It's amazing technology. I've never seen anything like it before. It's actually more powerful than a nuclear reactor. The thing could power a small city if it needed to. It's amazing. The applications for this are limitless. I can power up our grenades. Diana and I have already started working on supercharging PECs for increased size and duration. She even had an idea for using it to counter blast waves on a citywide scale. She thinks we can take another shot at saving the cities in the first campaign."

"That could be fun. So that's why you haven't been in here practicing for the last few days? I thought you'd finally given up on wanting to be a field agent."

"I'm never giving up."

"Are you here to shoot?"

Griz paused for a moment with a look of unease and scorn on his tired, dirty face. "Yes," he finally answered.

"Good, go get geared up and take the spot next to Nac. Maybe you'll learn a thing or two watching him." Nac sat up and reloaded his weapon. It was a rifle a bit smaller than an M-16 and weighed only six pounds even fully loaded with a full thirty-round magazine and three grenade rounds. He grabbed a full magazine from the pile on the ground at his station, ejected the empty cartridge, and loaded his weapon with the new magazine. Grom returned to his spot at the controls of the virtual targets while Griz ran over to the weapons wall.

Nac stood and rested his weapon against the wall of his booth and watched Griz. The smaller man grabbed a massive weapon from the rack. The weapon had two separate barrels stacked vertically. The first was a larger than normal rifle-sized barrel, finished off with a grenade launcher. Atop the top rifle barrel sat a large sniper scope elevated a full inch above the barrel, giving access to the standard metal sights for close combat.

Attached to the right side of the weapon was another small electronic device. Griz toggled it quickly off and on. A red laser shot out from the sight indicating an additional sighting option. The stock of the weapon had another large electrical panel on top just behind the rear metal sight. Griz hung the weapon by a strap over his shoulder and walked over to the ammunition case. He visibly strained under the weight of the weapon as it threw off his gait.

Nac watched in amusement as Griz grabbed several grenades, a box of .25 caliber ammunition, and several magazines. He walked back to the line of firing stations overlooking the range and unloaded all of his ammunition onto the table. He groaned as he removed the weapon from his back and leaned it against the station. Breathing heavily, he clicked a rifle magazine into place and loaded three grenades into the launcher. He raised the weapon to standard port arms. His arms trembled from the heft of the weapon. "Ready," he said with a determined look.

"We'll start with long range." Grom's voice boomed from the command console. A target shimmered into view at the far end of the range. Nac shifted into his firing position and released a single round. The target distorted and vanished. Three more targets appeared, and Nac quickly dispatched two, saving one for the younger man. Nac looked up noticing Griz struggled to move his weapon to keep in line with the moving target. He tensed, and fired.

The rifle kicked against the frail boy's shoulder, shoving him backward and spinning him clockwise. The scope smacked his visor, crushing the glass and slamming into his face. He dropped the rifle to the ground. It spun to aim toward Nac but didn't fire again. "Oh My God." He screamed, clawing at his face with this hands. He popped the visor off and dropped it to the ground. He removed his hand slowly, revealing a large red circle around his eye. A small shard of plastic was lodged in front of his ear. A single tear rolled down from each eye.

Nac laughed. “Hold still.” He reached out and pulled the shard of plastic from Griz’s face, dropping it to the ground. “You ever been punched in the face before?”

Griz shook his head, still rubbing his eye with his left hand.

“There’s a spot right on the nose. No matter how hard or gently you get hit, it’ll make you tear up every time. So, don’t sweat it. I did that my first time firing too. I assumed Grom taught you how to hold a rifle. My mistake.”

“First, get something smaller. Imagine carrying that beast on a long mission. Every ounce of weight is a burden. Ounces equal pounds, and pounds equal pain. Besides, the extra firepower is mostly wasted.”

“Good point,” Griz replied. The two continued their training for several hours until chow time. As they exited the range, Griz sheepishly looked to the older man.
“Can I get your advice on something? I meant to ask at the party, but things got a little crazy.”

“Sure, what’s up?”

The two entered the hallway leading to the dining facility. Griz walked quietly for a few moments, looking down at the ground. After several steps he finally took a deep breath and looked to Nac without breaking stride. “So, there’s this girl. I like her, but I don’t exactly know what to do.” His eyes timidly dropped back to the floor and darted about the plain concrete walkway. He reached up with his right hand and ran it through his hair. “I mean, how do I get her attention?"

Nac wrapped his arm around Griz and pulled him into his side in a shoulder hug as they continued to walk to the back of the line for food. “Well, it’s a bit tough here. You can’t exactly ask her to dinner and a movie. I also wouldn’t exactly suggest taking her on a romantic dinner to the chow hall. Does this place have a name, or is it just the dining area?"

"It's called Armano Hall after a field agent who sacrificed his life in San Francisco during the first campaign."

"Good to know. Anyways, Armano Hall isn't exactly a romantic spot. What does she like?" he asked. They reached the back of the line and waited.

"We grew up together. She was already here when I arrived. She was a year younger than I but always helped out with Arwen. We'd always run through the halls and explore the compound together. These days she works in the engineering labs and helps keep this place operational."

"Okay, that's great stuff to know, but not what I asked. What does she like?"

Griz paused for a moment. "Flowers?"

Nac laughed and shook his head. "Okay, I can help. let's get our food and we'll figure something out over lunch." Griz stepped off to the side and had the short order cook make him a cheeseburger while Nac went to the back of the ordering area. He grabbed three rolls of sushi, a wad of wasabi, and soy sauce. He then walked over to the fridge and grabbed two mason jars of Sweetness and headed out to the dining area. He found an empty table and grabbed a seat, waving Griz over as he left the food lines.

Griz joined him with a giant smile plastered across his face. "Okay, when we were younger we always used to go roller skating together at the far end of the compound in the recreation areas."

"Perfect. Steal some flowers from the rec areas, take her roller skating and surprise her with the flowers somewhere. Boom, you've got a date."

“How do I ask her?" Griz asked, then paused, noting a pained look on Nac’s face. His eyes watered and his jaw tensed as though biting down in anger. He closed his eyes and exhaled deeply through his nose. “Are you okay?"

Nac didn’t answer for several seconds. His eyes remained closed. His breath sounded loud and deep through his nose as if in meditation to control his senses. After a few moments he opened his eyes. They watered, but he smiled. “Yeah, just got a big hit of wasabi. I love it when that happens. Anyway, when’s the last time you saw her?"

“A few days ago. We don’t spend as much time together as we used to."

“Well, next time you see her just make a point to schedule a time to go skating together. Don’t overthink it. By the way, what’s her name?”

“Chara. What do I do to make her like me?"

“From what you said, it sounds like she already does, right?”

Griz nodded. “I guess."

“Good, then just be yourself and don’t do anything stupid. It’ll all work out. If you run into a strange situation and aren’t sure how to act, just ask yourself how a good man would handle the situation, and do that. You can’t go wrong."

He smiled and looked over to Nac. “Thanks. I think you’re right. Now I just have to figure out how to get flowers without her finding out."

“If that’s your biggest challenge you shouldn’t have any problems."

“Problems with what?" Diana asked, walking up to the table with a tray full of food. She smiled down at the two men and placed her tray down on the tabletop. Nac immediately stood and walked over to her. He pulled her forward by her hips with both hands. Her body pressed against his chest in a tight hug. He leaned down and gave her a soft kiss. "Hey, you sexy beast."

He pulled out her chair and moved around behind it. He waited for her to sit, then returned to his seat beside her. He looked over at her as she settled in. She wore a pair of blue jeans and a green tank top, matching green shoes with a small heel. Her hair was still a vibrant red and matched her ruby red lips.

"I was just giving Griz a little advice. I guess he saw how irresistible I am to you and knew I was the best choice for counsel. He's got his eye on a girl and wants to take her out. I told him to make sure she looks as good as you do in flats."

"Don't get too cocky," she replied, with a sharp glance and a smile. "What's her name? Is it anyone I know?"

"Chara. I think you work with her down in engineering."

"Oh Chara! She's going to be great. She's a natural and is learning quickly. She's way ahead of where I was at that age, and she's super cute. You two will look great together. When's the big date?"

"I haven't asked her yet. Nac said I should wait until I see her, then propose we go skating. We used to skate together as kids. I'm also going to try and, well, we'll see how it goes."

"That sounds sweet, but don't wait. Go after her if that's what you want. Prince Charming over here probably forgot to mention that he waited for me to make the first move. Oh, before I forget, Dr. G. needs all three of us in the command center after lunch. He wants to get the next step going with the senator. If you feel ready, that is."

"I'm good to go, Alum cleared me for operations yesterday," Nac replied. "And I'm glad you think I'm charming."

"I was being sarcastic."

"That's not what I heard."

The trio quickly finished eating, packed up, and walked out of Armano Hall back toward the command center. As they walked in, Griz waved to his sister Arwen sitting in the back corner. She didn't even look up, unaware of the new arrivals. She was focused on the screen in front of her. Her frame was mostly blocked by her workstation, but Nac could see her dark brown hair was pulled back into a ponytail and the monocle sat prominently over her left eye. Puffy white sleeves popped out from under a rigid red over-shoulder corset.

They walked forward to see Dr. G. working with Vine at a nearby workstation while Alum patiently waited off to the side. Dr. G. was his normal self. He wore red thong sandals with nantucket red shorts and a white short sleeve silk shirt. Alum was her equally conservative self in her white pants and jacket over a dark yellow blouse with a deep v-neck.

Vine on the other hand looked like Spike Lee on a good trip. His dark dreadlocks streamed down from underneath a swirling lavender patterned fedora. He wore a shiny silver vest. His wrists were adorned with lavender bands which matched vertical lavender-striped long pants and bright silver shoes. Vine turned to Nac and smiled. "I'm excited for this mission," he stated as the group approached.

"Why's that?" Nac asked.

"You'll see."

"We're sending you to 2067. The senator will introduce you to his grandson, George R. Shaw, who is currently a congressman and a major player in politics. He's going to be carrying the torch going forward," Dr. G. stated. He then brought up an information readout on the screen displaying the senator and his grandson with their personal details.

"The senator, or as he's now known, the former President of the United States, is visiting his grandson in Washington, D.C. They're both going to speak with the K Street lobbyist firm, Ratlef and Webster. The firm is about to begin lobbying for the trading changes of the human fund that enabled Terra Futures. While Marcus has already created a legal exception to the futures trading of the human fund, Ratlef and Webster will continue using its influence to have the law rescinded. They succeed in changing political opinions over a five year period. We aren't sure who's funding their campaign."

"Marcus is currently one hundred and five years old, but he's still pretty sharp. His grandson, George, is forty-nine years old and has a bright future ahead of him. You'll make contact with them before they head into Ratlef and Webster, provide security for the mission, and see if you notice anything suspicious about the company. We don't expect any NP involvement.

"We mainly want you to thank Marcus for all of his work and make introductions with George. We need his help going forward. Nac, you'll need to change clothes to something a bit more appropriate for the times. You'd stand out like a sore thumb dressed like that. Vine, take care of him."

"Yes sir," Vine stated and moved off toward the polybox in the corner of the command center. Nac paused for a moment then walked inside the device. He stood in the low light of the small booth and waited until he heard the familiar hum of the machine coming to life, indicating that Vine had finished entering data. His clothes melted away leaving him naked for a moment. He glanced at the tattoo quickly on his right butt cheek. It was two green feet, five toes apiece, with a thin yellow outline. As he looked down he felt pants materializing around his legs and a fitted shirt forming on his torso.

He looked in the mirror to see shiny black loose fitting pants with matching shoes, and a dress shirt with three inch thick horizontal lavender colored stripes. He glanced down and noted the soles of his shoes had a matching vertical lavender stripe pattern.

"You gotta be kidding me," he stated with a hint of disdain in his voice as he stepped out of the tailoring station.

"You look great," Vine replied with a laugh.

"What's with the lavender anyway? How did it become popular?"

"In the early twenty-first century it was a symbol for gay rights.

"Wait, what?" Nac interrupted, "Lavender, not the rainbow?"

"Apparently just before gay rights went fully mainstream, Marvel Comics fans culturally appropriated the rainbow to honor their devotion to Stan Lee. Religious freedom triumphed over gay rights in court."

"Where was I, oh, yes. The lavender became the primary symbol for human rights. A few designers began making clothing with the colors stitched into discrete locations, and it took off. It was a fashionable way of saying you supported human equality."

Nac shook his head and rejoined the rest of the group near the transport pad. He looked to Diana whose mouth twisted into a restrained smile. She quickly raised her hand up to her face to cover her laughter as she read the embarrassment on Nac's face and turned away. She turned back to look at him and lowered her hand. "It's a good look for you," she replied, still stifling her smile.

"We have you jumping directly into the congressman's apartment in southeast D.C. It's the same apartment where you originally contacted Marcus in 2015," Griz stated as he handed each man their transport wristbands. "We'll have you arrive at ten AM. The meeting is at the headquarters of Ratlef and Webster at noon."

Vine and Nac nodded and stepped up to the platform. They turned around to face the team and nodded to Griz who raised his hand.

3,

2,

1,

Griz keyed the jump terminal. The last sight Nac saw as the compound vanished was the condescending smile on Diana's beautiful face. The men staggered as they found themselves an inch off the ground in the DC apartment. They quickly gathered themselves and surveyed the room, noting that not much had changed since their last visit.

A man sat on the large brown couch in the same seating area. He had a large headset covering his head to include his eyes and ears. He appeared oblivious to their arrival. He wore a sharp black suit with a lavender print tie. The inside of his suit bore a matching bright lavender lining.

Nac and Vine turned quickly as they heard the toilet

flush to their back right. They listened and waited as the water faucet turned on moments later. The door finally opened and an old man in a wheelchair rolled out to the main room. He wore a navy blue suit with a white dress shirt underneath and no tie. His brown dress shoes bore the dull shine of polish. As he exited the bathroom his face lit up. “You two look exactly the same,” he said, running his right hand through his thin white hair. “It’s been too long."

“Marcus?”

“In the flesh. You don’t recognize me? Do I look that different?"

“No, not at all," Vine replied quickly. “You look great.”

“Bullshit, but thanks."

“Well, let me introduce you to my grandson, George." He gestured to the man on the couch still engrossed in his headset. He wheeled himself past the bar and tapped his grandson on the leg who startled for a moment, then removed the headset. Seeing the new arrivals, he stood, buttoning his suit jacket. “Sorry, I didn’t hear you come in. I’m George." He stated as he reached his right hand out. “I assume you must be Vine and Nac?”

“I’m Nac and this here is Vine. And no worries. We didn’t exactly knock,” Nac replied, returning the handshake.

“I’ve heard a lot about you. My grandfather raised me on lessons of what he’s fighting for and in recent years has described the mission to me. I’m excited to do my part and carry on his work."

“We’re lucky to have you,” Vine replied, turning toward Marcus. “Marcus did great work with us. We’re better off because of him. We believe you can keep us moving forward. We know this plan will work. We just need to keep going. We'll keep you aware of any problems that arise in the future. You just keep the plan on track here."

"Easy enough. Any chance you can tell me if I win the presidential election in 2084?"

"Maybe. We can look into it, but the outcome can always change. Look, we're here for today's mission. We want to not only remove Ratlef and Webster as a negative force on our mission, but also to hire them to lobby on our behalf."

"The ol' switcheroo?" Marcus interrupted. "That won't be a problem for these people. They have no loyalty. We'll just have to pay them more than our competition."

"That can be arranged, within reason."

"How?" George asked.

"There are some advantages to being time travellers. We play the markets just enough to avoid influencing them while still being able to fully fund our missions."

"Let's start heading over. We don't want to be late in case there's traffic," George replied.

"No future engineer has solved the traffic problem yet?" Nac asked.

"Not yet. Maybe after we save the world we can solve that problem." George replied. "The hardest part is upgrading the existing cars. You can't force a family that just bought its first car to get a ten thousand dollar upgrade. I suggested we buy all the cars not worth upgrading, replacing them with climate friendly models, and having a globally broadcast world's largest demolition derby with the remainder to pay for it. Gramps didn't bite. He said it didn't sound professional enough."

The men shared an elevator ride down to the parking garage and loaded into the car. George took special care to assist Marcus into the front seat and loaded his wheelchair into the trunk. He hopped into the car and started the ignition. The car rose slightly. Nac startled and quickly looked around. "Flying cars?"

"Not exactly," George replied as the car began to move. "Most roads are magnetic now. We're just floating a few inches off the surface. It provides better control and has eliminated almost all accidents. It also better enables self-driving and reduces wear on the road surface since there isn't any direct contact or friction. We've built in solar generators to the surface levels. It apparently has reduced city temperatures in the summer by upwards of five degrees, and our cities are now entirely solar powered."

Nac nodded and looked out the window at the changed D.C. cityscape. Every building was a nearly identical fourteen stories in height. The capitol building was still the tallest building in the city. The men weaved through the dense traffic of the inner city and quickly reached K Street. Arriving at their destination, George luckily found a parking spot near the entrance of the building. He stopped directly to the side of the spot and the car moved horizontally into the space.

The car lowered and came to a rest on the ground. The men gathered their belongings and stepped out. Marcus rose onto his legs and held onto the vehicle, waiting while George brought him his wheelchair. They gathered on the sidewalk and followed George toward a large building. The exterior was a mix of shiny metal and massive tinted windows. George pushed Marcus forward and into the K street office.

Nac entered the main lobby and looked up at the

cavernous room. It rose at least five stories in height, contrasting the claustrophobic feel of the overbearing buildings lining the narrow streets outside. A majestic bronze statue of a cavalry officer, sabre at the ready, atop a rearing horse dominated the center of the space. Several individuals sat on attached benches surrounding the statue.

The entire lobby, including the floors, appeared to be made of solid marble. There was not a single stray piece of litter anywhere in the room. A massive marble staircase sat in the back of the lobby and several elevators were to the side of the staircase. Two large black security gates with at least twelve security personnel prevented any unauthorized access.

Before the men could reach the security officer station, a man in a dark grey business suit approached them. The only item that had any personality was the double flag pin on his lapel. The leftmost flag was the American flag while its counterpart to the right was a solid lavender. "Mr. President, it's great to see you again," he stated, reaching out to shake Marcus' hand. After a quick exchange of pleasantries the man identified himself as Kyle Ratlef, son of the founder of the business. Quickly the four men received access badges and moved into the elevator. They rose to the top floor and entered a large meeting room.

The focus of the room was a large polished wooden table with at least thirty chairs tucked neatly around the edges. Several bottles of water sat on the table along with bagels and assorted fruits. Colorful paintings lined the walls and the floor had opulent sky blue carpet with no blemishes. As everyone took their seats Marcus wheeled himself to the foot of the table and addressed the group. "Let's be quick. You know why we're here."

"I think so," Kyle replied. "Why don't you tell me so I can be sure we're on the same page."

"We want you to drop your current client lobbying for options trading of the human fund and instead take up our position that it's a protected fund with special trading regulations. Futures trading, options trading, and any form of shorting of the stock are expressly illegal."

"I understand; however, as you said, our current client is paying us to argue his side. We can't exactly get a reputation for dropping clients when another opportunity arises."

"You don't have to. You can say you realise the error of your ways and want to do the right thing. It'd be even more convincing if you don't accept payment from us."

"We have a strict, no-pro-bono policy here at Ratlef and Webster," Kyle replied impassively. "However, you can convince us to change our stance on the matter."

George interjected, "We're prepared to pay you fifteen million dollars per year and you'll develop connections not only with my grandfather, but with me. I'm someone you'll want on your side in the future. This is your only chance to be on my good side."

Kyle paused for a moment. He looked to George, then to Marcus, and finally to Nac and Vine. He appeared to be weighing their faces, wondering if he could get more money. He turned his back to the men for a moment. The men sat in silence, staring at the back of his finely tailored suit. The stitching was meticulously done and showed fine craftsmanship. Kyle kept his back to the group, enjoying the control of the situation for nearly a minute of silence. He then turned to face George. Pausing again, he looked up. "You've got a deal."

"Outstanding," George replied. He stood to cement the deal with the shake of a hand. "One last thing. Who was paying you to lobby against us?"

"You know I can't tell you that."

Marcus snidely interjected, "You don't think we need to know that information to work with you and make a good plan of action going forward?" He looked to his grandson "We're wasting our time trying to deal with these guys."

"Look, I worked with a lawyer who represented his client. I can tell you the lawyer was named Leck Petersen." Vine startled in his seat, nearly knocking over his glass of water on the table. He bolted upright in dismay, head turning toward Kyle. He leaned forward and placed his elbows on the table. He looked up to Kyle then down to the ground. His eyes narrowed and showed pure rage. His jaw clenched. His hands clenched into fists atop the sturdy wooden table.

Oblivious to Vine's shift in demeanor, George smiled and stood. "We'll be in touch to iron out the details. Can you be in South Carolina the Saturday after Thanksgiving? We have a box for the Carolina - Clemson game. You should come down and join us. Bring Mr. Webster and a few guests if you'd like. Family is invited, too. Since we'll be working together in the future, we'd like to get to know you better."

"We'll be there," Kyle replied and shook Marcus' hand firmly.

The men stood and headed back outside to the elevator. George pushed Marcus while Nac drank lazily from a bottle of water he scored from the conference room. He casually strolled into the back of the elevator and took his place beside Vine. Nac could feel tension emanating from Vine, and his face seemed drained of blood. His hands clenched and unclenched sporadically.

Nac looked at him curiously, but maintained his silence. He absentmindedly rubbed the rally towel bulge in his right pocket to assuage his nerves. Upon reaching the lobby they shook hands with Kyle and quickly exited the pristine lobby. Nac stopped when they reached the car. "Before we head home I need to make a stop nearby. We'll be on our own from here," He stated to George and Marcus. Vine didn't even look to him in acknowledgement. He appeared lost in thought. Anger and sorrow battled in his eyes. "We'll meet you in South Carolina for the game. It'll be a great opportunity to speak with you more and try to get more information from the lobbyists."

The men exchanged goodbyes and Nac watched the Shaw family drive off. He then checked his wrist map for local shops and began walking down the street. Vine followed silently. He appeared completely lost in thought. He followed Nac blindly, like a small child or a lost puppy. Nac found his destination and paused. "Wait here, I'll be right back." Vine looked up but gave no indication of his awareness. He waited on the sidewalk for Nac to return. A few minutes later Nac popped back outside and the two men strode behind the building to the back alleyway.

"Ready?" Nac asked, with his hand behind his back. Vine nodded, barely looking up, and keyed their jump. The back alley of the Capitol Hill shops quickly changed to the drab white walls of the compound. Nac looked up with a smile, keeping his hand behind his back. Alum quickly ascended the stairs and cleared the duo. Nac remained on the stage until he locked eyes with Diana. He paused for a moment. A giant smile appeared on his face. With everyone's attention he walked down the steps toward her, silently, keeping his hand behind his back. She looked at him with a confused expression and stood, waiting.

"I have a little surprise for you," he stated with a sly smile as he came to a stop two feet in front of her.

She looked up at him with a curious hesitance, brushing her scarlet hair to the side of her right eye. "What is it?" She leaned to her right a bit, then back to the left, straining to see what he was hiding.

He pulled his hand from behind his back revealing a beautiful bouquet of roses, six white and six pink. She smiled, mouth open and white teeth shining in the fluorescent lighting. She surged forward and wrapped herself around Nac. He matched her speed, holding the flowers out to his side to avoid crushing them. She looked up and he relented. He leaned down so she could kiss him. He felt his world slow down. He heard Dr. G. say something, but didn't make out the words.

She pulled back, her hands sliding off Nac's shoulders. He felt a lingering warmth. She looked up to his eyes. "No one's ever bought me flowers before."

"I'm glad you like them. I told you I'm charming," he replied with his same smile still plastered across his face.

"You have your moments," she answered and took the flowers from him. She held them to her nose and inhaled deeply, glancing to Alum as Nac turned around. His smile faded as he looked back to his sullen partner.

"Vine, are you okay? You've been acting strangely."

Vine looked back to Nac. He paused, then, in barely a whisper, spoke the word, "Leck."

Nac looked at him in confusion, but noticed Diana,

Griz, and Alum all snapped their heads upright to focus on Vine. The smile was gone from Diana's face, replaced by a look of terror. She lowered the flowers to her side, parallel to the floor. Alum's face became pale, as though she'd seen a ghost. Griz ran his hand through his spiky hair, eyes closed as he clenched his jaw. Even Dr. G. froze, then reached up to rub the jagged scar bisecting his right eye.

"What does that mean?" Nac asked in confusion.

Vine paused, slowly looking to the rest of the team, then back to Nac. He took a deep breath. "Leck is Mal."

Chapter 9

Several days later, still at the compound, Nac woke and completed his morning routine. He rolled past Diana, shaking her enough to wake her. Six sun salutations later he walked out ready to go, while she searched frantically for a cup of coffee. They ate in near silence. Diana barely took a bite of her food, poking at it slowly without looking up. She had dark circles under her eyes as though she hadn't gotten any sleep. Nac devoured his food and drank his usual two glasses of sweetness. After only a few minutes the two walked off together toward the command center.

Upon arrival they saw Griz and Dr. G. already present with Alum in her usual position near the platform. She already had her full medical case at her feet. A large red cross was emblazoned on the top.

Dr. G. was in his all too familiar sandals white short sleeve silk shirt, and khaki shorts. He seemed his usual relaxedly uptight self. Griz was dressed like a college kid. He wore a garnet short sleeve shirt with 'Carolina Football' written across the chest in two lines. Long white sleeves streamed out from underneath the short sleeve shirt. He also wore a pair blue jeans and standard brown shoes.

Nac heard the door of the tailor slam shut with an excessive metallic clang. Vine stepped out, oblivious or unconcerned of his clamor. He walked past a man and woman standing in line in front of the station awaiting their chance to get new clothing. Vine walked over to the group wearing a garnet long sleeve rugby shirt with a gamecock logo over the right chest and black pants with black shoes. "These assignments just keep improving. G, I definitely support the decision to move on from the first campaign."

"G?" Nac bemused.

"I knew him before the promotion."

"Just keep your mind on the mission," Dr. G. interrupted. "I don't want you two drinking on this one. Remember, we expect Mal to try to take out Congressman Shaw during the game. This has him written all over it. He loves public displays of violence."

Nac nodded and joined the woman waiting in line at the tailor as he saw the man step inside. After a few moments the man stepped out wearing khaki pants and a short sleeve garnet polo with a gamecock logo emblazoned on the left chest. He introduced himself to Nac as Tark. He stood at a modest height of only 5'7" but looked fairly fit. He had a full dark brown beard with a few white hairs and matching mustache. His hair was slicked back and fell to about shoulder length.

The woman stepped out of the tailor wearing a sharp black dress and garnet wedge heels with a two inch heel. She had tanned white skin and dark black hair, pulled back with a garnet headband. Her hair fell neatly behind her to her lower shoulders. She had matching garnet beaded bracelets on each wrist and garnet fingernail polish. With her heels she appeared an inch taller than her companion. She paused as she stepped out and affixed a gamecock sticker with a block C Gamecock logo to each cheek.

She introduced herself as Sabby. Holding open the door of the tailor to Nac, her hand slid across Nac's arm as he entered. Her eyes looked to Diana with contempt.

Nac took the moment to step inside and configure his mission attire. After the all too familiar feel of the booth modifying his clothes, he stepped back out. He wore a clean white polo shirt, garnet sleeves poking out from underneath. He also wore nicely tailored white and garnet seersucker pants with a black belt which gently broke onto black shoes. He quickly walked over to Dr. G. who appeared to be impatiently awaiting his arrival to begin the brief.

"Okay, let's get started." He keyed up a map of the football stadium and the immediate surrounding area. "This is Gamecock Park. You'll meet up with the Shaw family at their tailgate on the east side of the stadium. They have a permanent spot in the second row here." He indicated a spot on the map labeled thirty seven.

"Your mission is simply to provide protection for the congressman, his family, and the lobbyists. Given your longstanding relationship with the Shaw family, Nac and Vine will be in the tailgate. Sabby and Tark will stay on the perimeter and try to spot anyone coming who looks suspicious."

Dr. G. keyed up an image on the screen of a man's face. He had a strong jawline and a clean shaven face leading up to tightly cut black hair. Brown eyes stared out from the screen at the onlookers. The eyes burned with anger. The lips seemed poised to snarl. The face conveyed a combination of scorn and supremacy. "This is Leck Petersen, aka 'Mal'. He was in direct contact with the lobbyists who are now helping us. That makes them enemies to him. His enemies don't usually live long. That's another reason we expect him to make an appearance. Everyone working against him will be in one place.

"You may notice Griz is dressed to go on this one. He's going to set up his own spot near the tailgate and coordinate communication and electronic surveillance for you all. He'll be out of sight the entire time. Diana will be remaining here per the protocol between herself and Griz. Any questions?"

Dr. G. paused and looked around the room. Everyone stood tall, looks of determined resolve showed on each face.

"Good. Remember, Mal is the most dangerous agent we've ever faced. He usually works alone, and he usually chains pretimed jump sequences. Keep your guard up at all times. There will be a lot of activity going on around you. It will be impossible to maintain control of the situation if things get out of hand. Don't try. Focus on the mission, and good luck."

"Hey G. Remember that time you said to shoot everywhere but where he was? Think this'll get that bad?" Vine asked.

"Every once in a while, I agree with Diana. You do talk too much," he replied.

All five members of the jump team smiled and grabbed their backpacks. They quickly ascended the platform, walking past Alum. She waited at the base of the platform. The medical kit at her feet seemed imposing and out of place. She looked at them with a hint of fear and worry.

As Nac stepped past Dr. G. he was grabbed on his bicep by the older man. He leaned into Nac's ear, and whispered so no one else in the room could hear. "Do me a favor. Don't try to confront Mal alone. Keep your cool. When you see him, expect an ambush. Don't attack for once."

Nac paused, and looked to Dr. G. in silence. He then turned and walked back to Diana. He wrapped his arms around her and pulled her tightly against his body with both hands. His hand slid down and grabbed her ass.

"Just in case." He turned and walked back to the platform.

Griz raised his hand.

1,

Alum looked to Dr. G. Her eyes were wet. Her face clenched in a frown. Her hands trembled.

2,

"See you in thirty seconds," Nac stated confidently. His eyes conveyed focus and purpose on the mission ahead. His jaw was clenched, showing his tense nerves at whatever awaited him in Columbia, South Carolina.

"No different than last night, I bet," Vine interjected.

3,

The members of the team waiting in the command center vanished along with its white walls. The five members of the forward team looked around to a small grassy area. The sky was a soft blue with a few fluffy white clouds. The temperature was a perfect seventy-five degrees fahrenheit.

They stood in a back yard of a large house contained by a tattered looking white wooden fence. The grass was mostly barren brown patches of dirt and poorly kept weeds. Beer bottles and cans littered the ground, intermingled with a few empty handles of liquor and burned cigarette butts.

A large heavily worn wooden table sat off to the side with several red solo cups and small ping pong balls scattered over the top and on the ground. To the edge of the lawn was a large brick home that looked solidly built and well kept. Three lawn chairs sat at the base. Each was occupied. One man and a woman were unconscious and snoring while the third looked at the new arrivals with bloodshot eyes. Nac was unsure if his shock was due to their presence, or his gut.

Nac smiled at them, kicking a beer can on the ground, before moving forward. The other four members of the team followed. They walked around the side of the house. As they reached the front lawn they looked back toward the large brick building. A few individuals sat on the front steps chatting away and sipping on various drinks. Three large greek letters hung in white wood over the top of the front entrance.

"Okay, it's eleven A.M. We have to be set up at the tailgate by two in the afternoon. Tark, Sabby, take Griz to secure a rental vehicle for your communications location in the park. Try to get an SUV to give Griz some concealment. Nac and I will go meet up with the Shaw family. Keep comms open," Vine ordered.

The rest of the team nodded and headed off on their respective missions. Nac and Vine moved toward the stadium. It was less than a mile from their location, and they moved down the sides of the road. A small trickle of other tailgaters also flowed in that direction. "Vine, what's the word on Mal? What's your history with him?"

They continued walking in silence for a moment

until Vine halted and turned toward Nac. His eyes were a watery red. Nac stopped and faced him. "Three down, five from the left."

"What do you mean?"

"Rana. That's her spot on the wall. We were infiltrating one of the NP bases with a large contingent of Bulwark agents. Something went wrong when we were breaching their perimeter. They had nothing but an overlapping concentric drone field.

"It's a swarm of miniature flying drones, evolved from racing drones hobbyist used. Each has a different sensor setting. Heat, electromagnetic, even active sonar. Each is programmed to go full kamikaze at any new readout. Once one goes, twenty five percent of the entire wave continues the barrage in perfect mathematical slaughter. It's unstoppable fire superiority.

"The first explosion was one hundred feet to our left. You don't want to know that feeling." He paused. "I jumped. When I jumped back, she'd been Redwooded. As far as the world knows, she never existed. Anyone who wasn't on that mission with me doesn't even remember her."

He reached into his pocket and pulled out a picture. It showed a slightly overweight woman with light brown skin. She had short curly hair and a giant smile. She held a fat orange tabby cat in a gentle hug. It burrowed into her dark navy blue sweater. The sweater fit her comfortably with a wavy fit and had a recurring pattern of five horizontal lines. The stripes formed a dusty palette navy blue divided rainbow.

"I know what they do to the women they take. He told me he'd personally handled her interrogation." He closed his eyes. "I'm still here. I'll get him."

Nac stood in surprise, stunned. After a moment he jogged after Vine to catch up. He reached Vine's side and wrapped his arm around the smaller man's shoulder. "I'm sorry," he stated as they continued moving forward.

They walked quietly for a bit longer until Vine finally broke the silence. "She was the most beautiful creature I've ever met, inside and out. She originally joined us after her parents were killed as collateral damage in a NP raid. When I joined The Bulwark I was assigned as her partner, even though she didn't want me.

"She was the best agent we had. Always quick on the trigger. Always made the right decision. Always looked out for her team. She always seemed so focused, because she knew the stakes. Then she'd surprise you with the kindest gesture. I remember she once brought me back some wine from a mission because she knew it'd make me happy. Back then the missions were much larger and more combat intensive. I couldn't believe she deviated from the plan for me."

"The first campaign?"

"Yeah. It was bloody. I'm lucky I survived." Vine paused for a moment, pain still lingering on his face.

"How'd you end up here?"

"Wrong place, wrong time, just not wrong enough."

"Anyone from your unit make it?"

"Yeah, but he died in his first mission with The Bulwark. His name was Alex. He was a great man. We went through boot at Parris together. We were on a fireteam together for five years."

"So he's on the wall also?"

"No, redwoods are reserved for those who were deleted from time. It's something other than a memory to show they existed. We don't have enough space to memorialize everyone who's ever gone down on a mission."

They continued to walk down the road, the crowd getting slightly thicker. A man rode by them on a scooter with a large cooler attached. He sat atop the scooter, feet occasionally brushing the concrete of the road beneath him. He navigated with one hand while another clutched a beer. A giant garnet sticker was affixed to the side of the cooler with the simple message, "Go Gamecocks." Nac watched him ride down the street, the stadium looming large in the distance. The man beamed with joy, occasionally cheering at random pedestrians, oblivious to the threat looming in the future.

"What did Dr. G. mean when he mentioned the protocols between Griz and Diana?" Nac asked.

"The jump calculation is complex. I've seen it, and it's just a jumble of weird greek shit to me. Math always kicked my ass. Anyway, Griz and Diana are the only two who've proven reliable at making the calculation. They're working on teaching some of the other engineers how it works. From my understanding it's a combination of advanced calculus and astronautical engineering. Not really sure though. Smart shit. They aren't allowed to jump at the same time for fear of losing them both."

Nac nodded as they continued forward. He looked around at the now much more dense crowd. Everyone was dressed in garnet. A few dots of orange and purple spotted the crowd.

"I've been working with Griz lately on improving our jump orientation. He's getting better."

The duo continued to weave their way through the crowd, occasionally bumping into careless partiers. They finally reached the base of the stadium. They moved around the edge of the coliseum, past several statues of legends of days past and into the tailgating area of Gamecock Park.

The first statue featured a large man standing alone on a bench looking forward. He wore full pads but carried his helmet by its face mask in his right hand. His smile seemed to be his most prominent feature.

Offset from the first statue was a large ring of colossal bronze figures. Each man wore full pads and a helmet. The men's gargantuan size made them appeare ready to compete in a rock throwing contest against André the Giant. The statues stood facing inward in a tight circle. From the center of the huddle a single fist emerged merely inches above the helmets of the hulking figures. The fist clenched a simple headset with the single word 'BOOM' engraved on each earpiece.

The large outdoor area was lined with cars concealed behind trees adorned with red and yellow leaves. The green grass lining the white concrete walkways was dotted with fallen leaves, adding additional color to the scenery. Music played loudly in all directions. The sound of the scattered crowd surrounded them in a low rumble of white noise.

The two men finally reached the tailgate area and saw George already setting up his tailgate in spot thirty-seven. He hastily placed out several items on tables in his space, tucked neatly under a tree full of vibrant red and yellow leaves. The first table held several types of booze and an ice luge for shots. Underneath that table were two coolers with transparent tops revealing beer filling one and assorted sodas in the second.

A large jug of water sat on the edge of the table. The second table was a line of homemade delicacies ranging from corn pudding to collard greens. Another cooler sat underneath filled with hot dogs and hamburgers. A few veggie burgers sat on top looking out of place amid the meat.

The congressman turned to greet them as they approached. He reached out a hand which Nac immediately walked up and shook, placing his other hand on George's shoulder. He looked at George wearing a garnet dress shirt with black pants and black shoes. "Thank you two for joining us. The rest of the Shaw clan is on their way. They should be here soon. Are either of you good with a grill?"

"I am," Nac replied quickly.

"Great, do you mind being the cook in a few when everyone gets here?" Nac simply nodded in reply. "Outstanding. There are burgers and dogs in the cooler."

The men all joined in to finish setting up the tailgate until they heard Griz's voice rattle in their ears. "We're en route. We secured an SUV and already purchased a parking spot in a nearby lot. It's less than a quarter mile from you. Hopefully we won't have any issues with comms with so many people in such a tight space. Our frequency isn't used by most hardware from this time so it shouldn't be an issue."

"Roger, let me know when you find your spot. I'll come locate you and get the rest of our gear," Nac replied.

"Will do."

The next hour passed uneventfully. Various members of the Shaw family arrived along with several powerful members of Washington D.C. ranging from politicians to reporters and lobbyists. George had three children, a boy aged thirteen, a daughter aged eighteen, and a son who was a junior at the University of South Carolina at age twenty-one. Each child arrived with several friends in tow hoping to enjoy the amazing spread put forth by the Shaw family. Marcus was one of the last to arrive, pushed across the open tailgating area in his wheelchair by the eldest of his great grand children.

The youngest generation was all dressed casually in jeans and garnet shirts with varied Gamecock slogans. Marcus showed up wearing a sharp all black suit with garnet lining, a white dress shirt, and a garnet tie with patterned gamecock logos throughout. The extended family was also present making at least thirty members of the Shaw family in all. Babies clung to mothers and toddlers rolled about in the grass. A few teenage boys tossed a football back and forth, occasionally interrupting a conversation as a missed catch rolled into someone's foot or bounced up to strike a leg.

Shortly after Marcus' arrival, Nac walked over to join Griz, Tark, and Sabby near the outskirts of the tailgating area. He quickly updated them on the size of the Shaw party with a brief description of each member present. Tark and Sabby headed off toward the tailgate to take up overwatch positions. As Nac turned to leave, Griz stopped him. "I got a date with Chara tonight."

"What's the plan, anything crazy exotic?"

"Actually, we're just going to take a stroll around the compound and go to the atrium to get some sun for a bit. She says she likes spending her time there these days."

"That sounds like a great idea."

"Yeah, thanks for the help."

"No problem. By the way, what's this I hear that you do all of our jump calculations? Is that true?"

"Yes."

"But when I first arrived you said you didn't know where we were."

"I lied. You had enough to worry about that day."

"Good to know I can trust you." Nac patted him on the back, re-hefted his small backpack, and walked back to the tailgate. Griz climbed into the back of the SUV and loaded his information readouts. It displayed locations of all team members as well as several additional points stacked on top of Nac's current location. His second screen displayed the security feeds of the stadium and from several stores in the area. The large blotch of locator points moved slowly but steadily toward the Shaw tailgate indicated by Vine's current location.

Upon returning to the group, Nac noticed that both Mr. Ratlef and Mr. Webster had arrived. Mr. Ratlef was wearing a simple blue shirt over jeans while Mr. Webster had on a lavender dress shirt and black slacks. Both wore American flag pins on their chests. After greeting the new arrivals, Nac discretely slipped the personal shields to Marcus, George, and his wife. He then took up his spot as grillmaster.

He chatted idly while flipping the burgers and listening to the chatter of those around him. Someone keyed a radio allowing the group to listen to the Iron Bowl. He looked around at other tailgates, noting the gatherings with televisions all sat in a line staring forward, while those listening to the radio sat in circles listening intently.

The day progressed without event. Delicious food and drink were had by all. Nac and Vine ate well, but refrained from the drinks. Marcus even stood at one point and took a shot from the ice luge while his great grandchildren filmed.

South Carolina was ranked twelfth and needed a win for a great season while Clemson was barely inside the top ten after losing a game in their weak regular season schedule. It would definitely be an intensely hard hitting game. Cheerleaders walked through the crowd handing out stickers and posing for photographs with families and young men hoping to get noticed. Cocky himself strutted through the ground with an escort of four dainty cheerleaders, garnet ribbons in their hair.

Finally, the time came for everyone to head inside. No alarms had been set off. The family packed up and moved forward to the stadium, George gently pushed Marcus in his chair. Tark and Sabby moved with the family, maintaining a hundred foot distance and keeping an eye out. They had been on alert for hours but maintained their focus on the vigil. Small Shaw children ran about haphazardly. The entire family, four generations of Shaws, was present. They moved as a unit toward the imposing Williams Brice Stadium before them.

After checking their tickets, the family quickly moved to their box. It sat at the perfect height and was situated on the forty yard line of the Gamecock sideline. They immediately opened the windows to let in the air and the sounds from the stadium. The inside of the box was beautiful.

Garnet carpet ran from wall to wall. The walls themselves were adorned with priceless Gamecock memorabilia ranging from a signed Steve Spurrier football to replica jerseys from the fire ants. A panoramic photograph of the stadium on gameday hung on one wall. A large spread of food sat in a corner with a bar nearby. A short bartender in a simple garnet polo stood behind taking orders. No tip jar rested on the bar before him.

The family settled in. Garnet was everywhere in the room. Nac shook his head at the lobbyists. Patriots through profit.

Nac and Vine grabbed waters from the bar then took seats near the front of the box to get a good view of the upcoming action below. Tark and Sabby took up positions on the concrete concourse outside. Both had perfect views of the entrance to the box. No one could enter undetected.

Nac heard a roar from the crowd below and stood. White rally towels waved in all directions. A wall of garnet roared. White towels flashed in circles above their heads. The noise built. Drums rang out. The noise built. Trumpets blared. The noise built. Bass of drums echoed through the stadium above the roar of the cheering crowd. The noise built. The noise reached a crescendo as the sounds of 2001 finished its buildup and the home team charged out from the tunnel. Smoke billowed around them. Flame spewed into the night sky. Players streamed forth in full garnet regalia to include garnet helmets. Crazed fans screamed.

Their cheers were broken by an even louder chorus of boos as the visiting Tigers took the field in orange pants and helmets with white tops. After a few minutes the game was set to begin. Electric energy could be felt throughout the stadium.

The sound of an explosion rang out. Vine startled and jumped to his feet. Nac jumped up as well, only in excitement as the cannon synchronized with kickoff. The ball sailed down the field as the kicker got the action started. "Spurs Up", rang out from everyone present. Marcus jumped from his chair. Only a few seconds later a wave of garnet crashed into orange, and brought the ball carrier down. The game was underway.

The contest quickly reached halftime with the score

all knotted up, thirteen apiece in a defensive, hard-hitting slugfest. Both teams had given it their all, and neither had prevailed in a matchup for the ages. South Carolina would get the ball to start the second half and looked to get the offense going again. Clemson's stout defense wouldn't be an easy opponent. The second half began. Cheers rang out through the crowd.

Carolina scored after a long, hard fought drive on the ground to take a six point lead. Everyone in the box cheered as the extra point sailed through the goal post. Smiles dotted the faces of everyone present. The techno song 'Sandstorm' blared over the loudspeakers. The stadium shook and swayed. Bass matched the pound of one hundred thousand feet impacting concrete superstructure.

Something seemed wrong, but in the euphoria of the crowd, Nac couldn't quite place it. He stood and meandered through the Shaw family. Everyone talked excitedly. Everyone was happy. As the kickoff was about to take place, Nac realized what was missing: Mr. Ratlef and Mr. Webster. He keyed his mic. "Does anyone have visibility on the lobbyists?"

Tark's voice came over the receiver. "They both stepped out to the bathroom a few minutes ago. I'm sure they'll be right back."

"There are bathrooms in the suite," Vine chimed in. His voice was tense. Silence filled the airways. The noise of the crowd sounded dull in the background.

"Tark, leave your post and find them. Sabby, stay put and tell me if anyone approaches the door. I'm going to warn Marcus and George."

The explosion of a cannon rang out. "Fight. Win. Kickass" echoed through the stadium. Nac walked up to

George standing beside Marcus, looking down intently at the play before him. The energized Carolina coverage unit rushed down the field and downed the Clemson returner at the seventeen yard line. The crowd roared in approval. White towels waved above a mass of garnet in a chaotic unity. He tapped the man on the shoulder. "Both of the lobbyists have disappeared."

"Where are they?" George asked as the crowd roared approval. The defense had stopped the play for a minimal gain.

"We're not sure, but we have one of our agents trying to locate them. I noticed neither of them brought any guests. Were they allowed to bring family and friends?"

"Yes, they were. I don't know why they came alone. Should we be worried?" Marcus asked.

"I'm not sure. We have one agent still watching the door so we should get any warning of activity, but your whole family is here. It's nearly impossible to protect everyone if the NPs make a move."

"Let's give it five minutes and see if they turn up."

Griz's voice echoed in Nac's ear. "I see them. I tapped into stadium security feeds. Both men just left the stadium, west side."

"Tark, intercept. Sabby, remain in your position. Stay alert. They could just be leaving early."

"No lobbyist has ever given up time with a former President and sitting member of Congress, much less everyone else in that room. This is priceless for them," Sabby interjected into her mic. Boos echoed from the field at a call by the referees.

"They're on the west side, about two hundred meters from the stadium. They've paused in a Bojangles parki--, holy shit. They just jumped!"

“Repeat last," Vine frantically commanded. The crowd roared again as the game continued. South Carolina had forced a punt to the delight of the crowd.

“They just jumped," Griz repeated. “They’re gone."

“Shit. Get everyone out of here now," Nac commanded.

Vine rushed across the room to Marcus and George sitting near a window looking down at the game below. He bumped into them, causing both men to startle and look up at the large Bulwark agent.

“Is there a problem?” Marcus asked.

“Yes. There’s no time to explain. Get everyone out, NOW!” Vine stated forcefully. Tark was already moving toward the door from his post at the outer concourse. Vine picked up a toddler and moved to the door as George stepped up onto a chair.

“Everyone, please listen up. We need to evacuate the room immediately,” he yelled to the room. A roar erupted from outside. The startled members of the room looked up, then slowly began moving toward the exit. Nac opened the door and grabbed a few men pulling them outside, much to their displeasure. Vine handed the toddler to a woman at the exit.

In under a minute roughly half of the party was safe. Tark sprinted to the door and stood with Nac just outside. They directed the scared Shaw family toward Sabby, who rallied everyone in a nearby alcove overlooking the twenty yard line. Only part of the field was visible from her post. The green grass sat in perfect tranquility. Play was on another part of the field. The intermittent roar of the crowd broke the low noise of the panicked Shaw family.

George still stood on his chair directing everyone to

leave as they slowly shuffled through the chokepoint of the entrance. Vine rushed to his side, reaching up to pull him from his perch and escort him to safety. Marcus approached the door in his chair and noticed a messenger bag sitting on the floor. It had a small logo consisting of three books in front of an American flag. The flag was held up by sabres on each side. The books were labeled on the seams with their titles; Freedom, Democracy, Sacrifice. The logo was that of Ratlef and Webster's firm.

He leaned down to pick it up. He keyed the clasp and opened the satchel, peering inside. The crowd roared. Sandstorm once again blared over the loudspeaker. The stadium itself shook as a hundred thousand fans continued their dance.

Marcus hurled himself out of his chair and onto the floor atop the bag. "Get back!" he screamed as he slammed into the ground. His wheelchair rolled backwards slightly and bumped into another family member. He clutched the bag firmly into his torso. Those still in the room recoiled backwards several steps. Those in the doorway scurried forward toward Tark. George stepped down from his perch. Vine moved forward to the prone President.

The room erupted.

Marcus was thrown upward at least a full three yards. The concrete ground below him opened up in a gaping hole of steel and concrete shrapnel. His body was engulfed in the bright blue light of his shield attempting to absorb the impact. He was torn to shreds. Screams echoed through the room. Family members were thrown back like rag dolls. Vine was tossed against the window overlooking the field. He slumped to the ground and landed on his side. Vine rolled to his back and passed out.

Nac turned as the concussive force ripped through the wall and triggered his shield. Nac's shield absorbed the impact that made it through the wall, but he fell backwards from the concussion force. Tark was not as lucky.

The open doorway happened to be at the exact line from the bomb to Tark's position. His shield couldn't handle the direct blast. Sabby sprinted over to kneel at Tark's side. The lower half of his body lay on the ground while the top half was atop a small crying child. Blood poured from several wounds all over Tark's lifeless body. Sabby rolled Tark to his back and pulled the small child into her chest. The child's howls rose, muffled by the fabric of Sabby's dress. Tark's body vanished only a moment later.

Several other members of the Shaw family lay in the doorway. Nac jumped over the body of a blonde haired woman laying in the threshold. Half of her face was gone. A large puddle of blood had already formed beneath her body, rapidly expanding outward. A small stream of blood ran off from the main puddle, underneath the blackened and charred remains of Marcus' wheelchair. It poured into the crater and onto the rubble below. Nac looked down through the crater and saw the lifeless body of the President crumpled atop large chunks of concrete. Steel bars stuck out of the corpse in random spots. The bodies of at least twenty fans lay crushed below the rubble, collateral damage.

Nac looked up, faintly hearing a voice in his earpiece, but ignoring it. He focused on the carnage of the room. He saw Vine lying on the ground. George knelt nearby hugging a crying girl who couldn't have been older than seven. A streak of blood was smeared on her left cheek over her Gamecock sticker. George pulled her against his chest. Her eyes were tightly closed, but her wails echoed through the room.

Nac ran to Vine's side and checked his pulse and breathing. Still alive, he moved to the next victim who appeared to have a chance at life, an older man Nac recognized as the senator from South Carolina. No pulse. Nac checked his airway, then performed CPR while giving rescue breaths. He watched the man's chest rise with each breath. He alternated between chest compression and rescue breaths. The body stayed still.

It twitched with each compression. The chest rose and fell with each forced breath. After a few more cycles, the man coughed loudly and moaned. Nac rolled the man onto his side, then sat back. As his butt hit his heels, he heard Griz's frantic voice in his ear. "Nac, Vine, did you hear me? Come in damnit! He's still approaching my vehicle."

Nac jumped to his feet and grabbed George. "Get your family to safety. I'm going after the fuckers who did this." George nodded, still clutching the girl in his arms. He rocked back and forth slightly in an attempt to comfort the distraught child. Nac paused, hand on George's shoulder, then ran outside. "Stay with Vine. Get him back safely," he screamed to Sabby as he ran past her. He paused to get his bearings and ran down the concourse. "I'm coming, Griz. Protect yourself until I get there."

Nac sprinted down the causeway now overflowing with fans in a panic trying to escape the stadium. The loudspeaker issued warnings of terrorist activity and instructed people to evacuate. Nac pushed his way through the crowd as fast as possible. People's faces were streaked with tears and looks of terror.

A man only ten yards from Nac fell. His scream of shock changed to pain as several other fleeing fans trampled his body. Other individuals tried to pull him to his feet, but the crowd surged forward in mass hysteria. Everyone was trying to survive and escape the unknown terrors at their backs. The crowd's inertia could not be stopped. Nac ran forward.

Struggling through the crowd, he reached the west exit. The crowd dispersed enough in the open area outside the stadium to allow Nac to sprint forward. "I'm almost there," he shouted to Griz through his microphone. He weaved through the dispersing crowd as quickly as he could. Small groups of people gathered together and attempted to regain their composure. They simply created a barrier Nac had to circumvent in his haste to reach Griz.

A soft explosion followed by Griz's scream sounded in Nac's ear.

Chapter 10

"Griz, report status," Nac yelled into his microphone. He ran forward, dodging members of the crowd scurrying away from the stadium. He weaved forward, hoping to hear Griz break radio silence. Nac ran along a line of cars and trucks. Litter from the festivities dotted the green grass of the tailgating area. A strong gust of wind ripped through the open air causing napkins to lift and spin. The breeze also carried sounds of worry and fear from the fleeing crowd.

Nac sprinted forward. The crowd lightened the farther he got from the carnage. He heard a groan in his ear and continued to run. "Vine is okay," Sabby's voice chimed in.

"Stay with the Shaw family. Get them to safety," Nac replied and kept running. He turned right and weaved between two tightly parked trucks, then an SUV beside a car. He stepped into the next open lane separating tailgate vehicles. He ran across the small strip of open space to Griz's SUV. The right side of the vehicle looked untouched. Nac ran around the side and skidded to a halt.

The left side of the car was a charred mess. The rear driver's side door was unhinged, destroyed. The door itself lay on the ground below, twisted and charred. Inside the car the seatbelt dangled from its top holster, but the band was shredded. Blood stains were smeared across the fabric.

At the front of the car Griz was crumpled to his knees, barely conscious. His head hung lazily, but sporadically popped up only to slowly sag once more. His mind struggled to wake up as his body shut down. His eyes were half open and appeared glazed over. His brown spikes were singed, and the left side of his face was covered in black charcoal. Blood ran slowly down his chin from his nose and mouth. His right leg was badly contorted. The knee was clearly broken. His arms slumped to his sides. A hand held his collar firmly, keeping him upright.

Nac took in the scene in a split second and appraised the man before him. One hand roughly held Griz while the other held a small device. Dark eyes stared forward with laser focus and zero compassion. His white shirt with purple tiger paw was streaked with blood and black ash. His jeans had smears of blood all over the left half where Griz's face had rubbed against the leg. Griz's laptop sat on the hood of the car to the side. The screen showed Griz's information readouts to include Nac's locator. He knew Nac was coming.

Mal.

"Hey lil' Willy," Mal snarled with a sinister smile.

Without pausing, Nac dove backwards behind the adjacent car. Mal keyed the device in his right hand. Both he and Griz vanished. Griz's rental vehicle erupted into an explosive fire tossing Nac backwards. Each adjacent car exploded a moment later. Nac was hit by the concussive force. His shield brightly surrounded him in a blue glow, stopping a large piece of shrapnel.

His flight backward was interrupted by the ground. He hit hard on his left shoulder and rolled against the grass, slamming into the front corner of a parked car. His spine bent back around the metal. The wind was knocked from his lungs. His head rang from the concussive blast. His vision was shaky and cloudy.

Nac rolled to his stomach and pushed himself to his feet. His head throbbed in agony and his ears rang. All sound was muted. He staggered several steps. He looked around at the carnage they created. Six cars in total were destroyed, another ten in surrounding parking places were ablaze and could explode at any moment. Several bodies littered the ground. Nac staggered forward toward the wreckage. Pain burned in his left leg. He looked down and saw a tear in his left pants leg above the knee. His blood was quickly darkening his seersucker pants.

A man ran past him. His face was bright red. He slid to a stop on his knees amid a cluster of bodies. Four children no older than ten lay crumpled together. Three bodies, two male and one female, lay intermingled with the children. Each was shredded by shrapnel and charred from the flames. The man howled in distress. He cradled one of the children's lifeless bodies against his chest. He looked up to the sky, wailing to the clouds, then back down, and buried his face against the blood-smeared scalp in his hands. He rocked back and forth, heaving as he sobbed.

Nac staggered over to the man and dropped to his knees at his side. He checked each of the bodies for signs of life, but found none. He began inspecting the man for damages, but he was unharmed. As his ears cleared he attempted to get the man's attention, but didn't receive a reply. The man kept rocking back and forth, cradling the lifeless body of the young child in his arms.

Nac stood and moved to a nearby cluster of people. A man and a child held the hands of a woman in a black dress. She lay on the ground, back resting against the chest of the man behind her. Blood smeared her black dress below her right ribs. Nac ran forward and slid to a stop beside her. He removed his polo then his long sleeve undershirt. He pulled out his knife and cut the front of the white polo shirt into six small squares, no more than five by five inches each. He dropped the rest of the tattered shirt while placing the six squares onto the woman's lap. He grabbed one and wiped away the blood from the wound.

"Hold this here. Keep pressure on it," he told the man, who quickly reached down. His face was pale from fear. Nac looked to the woman. Her breathing was rapid and shallow. Shock was evident in her face. Her eyes told a story of fear and pain. "It's okay. I'm an EMT. I'm going to stop the bleeding. You're going to be fine. Just keep breathing. Become Dory." He smiled.

The woman barely nodded and continued to breathe quickly. Nac cut his long sleeve undershirt sleeves off and tied the sleeves together. He moved the man's hand from the wound and covered it with fresh strips of white cloth from his polo. He tied the sleeves around the woman's waist to apply compression. "Hang tight. Help is on the way."

Nac moved to several individuals crumpled nearby and continued checking the bodies. Everyone was dead. Either the shrapnel or the concussive force, or both, were too much for the unprotected. At least thirty in total. Nac returned to the first man. He was still on his knees, leaning forward and pressing his mouth onto the forehead of the woman. He clasped her face between his palms, and he rocked back and forth. Moans and whimpers emanated outward. Nac slid to a stop beside the man and placed his hand on his back.

The man turned toward Nac and looked up. Bloodshot eyes stared at Nac atop a grime and blood-smeared face. Streaks of tears cut through the red and black mix of dirt and blood on his cheeks. "Are you okay? Are you unhurt?"

The man nodded. Nac relaxed for a moment, then stood and pulled the man to his feet. He stood 5'7" in a fitted black shirt with tight jeans and sharp looking black shoes. Everything was stained with smears of blood and dirt. The knees of his jeans were nearly solid black with bits of grass stuck to the fabric. He had black hair and a clean shaven face. His skin was a soft brown revealing his Asian heritage. "What happened? I was pulling my car out for my family to get in. What happened?"

"Terrorists," Nac replied, looking away from the man and toward the carnage surrounding them.

The man shook his head and dropped his face into his palms. After a moment he looked up, tears smearing the dirt, blood, and grime on his face. "How do you know?"

"I was here to stop them. I failed." Nac shook his head and looked at the wreckage around him. The flames on the vehicles were finally dying down. He ran his blood-stained hand through his hair. He felt weakness in his legs. His shoulders slouched. Burning gasoline and flesh assaulted his nose. Everywhere he looked was a mess of flames licking twisted metal. Spots of burning gasoline dotted the grassy walkways.

"Where did they go?"

Nac paused, finally taking a moment to let the events sink in. His eyes burned with anger. He stood tall, mentally vowing to get revenge. Mal would pay. "They're gone. You can't catch them right now," he replied as Sabby's voice chimed in on his headset. "Nac, are you okay? What happened?"

"I'm fine. They took Griz. We need to get out of here. How's Vine?"

"He's awake, but in pretty bad shape. I'm jumping back with him now. The congressman is safe. Marcus is dead."

"I know," Nac replied. "Get Vine home. I'll be there when you land."

The Asian man looked at Nac in surprise. "Are you going after them?" Nac paused, then nodded. "I want in," He said.

"That's not possible," Nac replied.

"Why not? I want revenge. I'm just a history professor, but I can be useful. It doesn't matter where they've gone. I can help you find them." He stood a bit straighter, a bit taller, and wiped the smears from his face.

"Okay, but there's no going back."

The man looked at him with a puzzled expression. "What do you mean?"

Nac paused, then smirked. "It's tough to explain. But when you get where we're going, just don't say anything. I'll look out for you. Definitely don't say your name."

The man nodded. "Come over here." Nac led the man between two larger cars and sat down. He reached into his backpack. He grabbed his jump band case and pulled it from the pack. He keyed in his code and opened the case. He grabbed a small partner jump band and held it out to his new companion. The man paused, looking to the bodies of his friends and family, then followed and crouched by Nac. "Put this on your left wrist."

The man took the band and slid it over his hand. It seated itself on his wrist and became snug. It glowed a soft red color. Nac returned the jump kit to his backpack and shouldered the pack. He keyed his wristband and watched. The man's band turned amber, then green. He looked back to the carnage around him one last time then reached down and pressed the jump button. The carnage vanished.

Nac staggered backwards as he appeared on the platform. Vine's prone body lay underneath his seat. Alum rushed forward to the stage and immediately began treatment on Vine. Sabby stepped down while the Asian man moved to the back of the platform in surprise, gripping his stomach. His face looked a sickly pale green.

"Who's this?" Dr. G. asked.

"A new recruit," Nac answered, kneeling next to Vine and giving him a pat on the shoulder.

The panic continued for a few more moments. Tark's torn body appeared in pieces on the platform beside Vine. Alum tripped over the new arrival and moved sideways, maintaining her focus on Vine. Tark's blood immediately pooled outward. The puddle expanded and pushed against Vine's leg. Alum finished with Vine, then turned to Nac to check his leg.

She focused on the task at hand, not allowing her emotions to betray her professionalism. Diana, standing at the jump console, turned away and hid her face. Her back trembled as she audibly sobbed. Dr. G's beard contorted. Even he seemed negatively impacted. After a moment Alum sat back on her heels still kneeling beside Nac. "Nac, Vine, you'll be fine but go to the medical bay.

I'll join you there to get you fully cleaned up." She looked down at Tark's lifeless body. Sadness showed in her normally serene eyes.

"Where's Arwen?" Nac asked.

"Who?" Alum replied, her face changing from focus to confusion.

"Redwood," Vine interjected flatly, standing and limping down the steps.

Alum closed her eyes and nodded, tears running down her cheeks as her defenses finally broke. She stood and moved to Dr. G. burrowing her face into his shoulder and wrapping her arms around his torso.

"Send me back!" Nac shouted. "Send me back to fifteen minutes before our return jump and I can save them."

"It doesn't work like that." Dr. G. replied, stepping away from Alum and towards the platform.

"How can you say that!" Nac slung his weapon and stepped down to the main floor. "How can you give up on them so easily!"

"Don't question me kid. This isn't my first rodeo. If this is a redwood" he turned and gestured to the wall of emblems "there's nothing we ca-" his words were cut short as Nac slugged him in the chin. He staggered backward and Nac moved forward grabbing the older man's collar. Vine reached out and grabbed Nac's arm. Alum stepped between the two men. Her face was bright red. Her nose and eyes were equally red and wet. Diana jumped in front of Nac and wrapped herself around him. Alum turned and shielded Dr. G.

"Calm down!" she shouted.

"You'll regret that." Dr. G. stated with surprising calm, rubbing his chin with a certain small smile on his face for the first time since Nac had known him.

"Both of you, Shut it." She interrupted, then wrapped herself around Dr. G.

Dr. G. looked down at the distressed woman in his arms. He locked eyes with her and whispered. He pulled her close. He squeezed her into his chest. "We'll get him back. I promise." He held her. The room sat in silence for a moment. "Diana, give the newbie his indoc."

Nac looked to the Asian man and nodded, then walked out with Vine and Alum, limping heavily. Vine walked gingerly as though in full body pain. He grabbed his left ribs with his right hand. Diana took a clipboard and headed off with the new arrival toward a debriefing room.

A few hours later Alum finished stitching up Nac. He walked out to the waiting area of the medical wing. As he exited he was greeted by Diana sitting there with the new companion. Both immediately stood when he limped into the room. Diana walked over and wrapped her arms around him, pulling him tight against her body. She stepped back, sliding her hands up his sides to his neck, and pulled him in for a kiss. "You scared me."

"I know, I'm sorry."

"I'm just glad you're okay."

"I am. Any word on Vine?"

"Vine will be fine. He has a few broken ribs and a concussion. He's staying in the medical ward for a few days under Alum's care. You'll have to work with her to put something on paper for, your friends. What were their names?

"Griz and Arwen. She was his sister."

Diana nodded. "By the way, meet Lammy," she said, turning to introduce the newest member of The Bulwark.

Lammy walked over to Nac and shook his hand. “It’s tough to explain may have been the understatement of the year."

Nac smiled and nodded. “I didn’t have time to spell it all out for you. What do you think?”

“I’m glad to be here. There’s nothing for me at home now. They killed everyone I cared about. I’m here to help. I’m here to win this.”

“I think he can help us in planning," Diana added. “Also, In spite of what happened yesterday, Dr. G. hasn’t grounded you. In fact, he wants to take you to control tomorrow. If you feel up to it, do you want to go?"

“Definitely. What should I expect?”

“It’s best if you see it for yourself. You don’t want to go into it with any expectations your first time,” Diana replied.

The next day Nac woke early and performed his usual ritual. He moved through his sun salutations and regained his footing, breathing a bit heavily. His leg ached from the wound sustained during his encounter with Mal. He walked out to Armano Hall and grabbed his breakfast in silence, then went to meet with Vine in his hospital bed. After a quick check on his friend, he moved to the command center and met up with Diana, Dr. G, and Alum. The two men exchanged a brief glance, then Nac turned to the redwood wall. Two workers were busy nailing two new emblems into the fourth row.

Diana quickly issued the two men PECs, which they clipped to their belts, and Nac realized for the first time that there was a new face behind the transport console. A young woman stood with short cropped blonde hair, and shiny green eyes. A light yellow sundress sat atop her pale skin. Her nose and cheeks were dotted with freckles.

The pair walked up to the platform. They turned to face the new girl standing with Diana and Alum. Nac looked down at the normally white platform. A large maroon stain blemished the back left corner.

"Chara, is everything ready for them to jump to control?" Diana asked.

"Yes, ma'am," she replied concisely.

She checked her readouts to confirm positive interface on the jump console and raised her hand.

3,

2,

1,

Nac, wincing slightly as though he'd taken a shot of Jameson, gazed around at the scene before him. He stood on a small hill overlooking a mostly clear area. Small patches of overgrown brown grass dotted the landscape which was otherwise completely barren. Brown dirt was the primary landscape. Large brown boulders dotted the horizon. No birds flew in the sky. No squirrels or animals ran about. A few small trees appeared to linger in the distance, but they were mostly barren. His PEC began to hum and vibrate against his waist as it revved up the power.

Upon closer inspection, Nac noted that the trees were all dead. Some were shattered and decomposing in the sun. He turned around to see a similar scene on all sides of the hill. To one side, a small stream trickled down a large dry brown crevasse at least three hundred yards wide. Between the hill and the stream lay a line of massive crumbled stones. Most of the boulders were an off-white color with intermittent dark black scorch marks blemishing entire faces of stone. The only sound was the breathing of the men, the whistling of the wind over the mostly unblemished landscape, and the soft hum of the PECs. The air was humid and full of dust. The sun beat down harshly from above.

Dr. G. broke the silence. "Radiation levels are high. Our PECs should give us twenty minutes of protection before we need to return. We won't be staying that long." Nac felt the battle between his PECs and the environment. He began to sweat heavily. Even though the temperature was regulated, the overbearing heat challenged the PEC barrier. "Current outdoor temperature is one hundred seventy-four degrees fahrenheit."

"Where are we?" Nac asked.

"You don't recognize this?"

"No."

"That's the Washington Monument." Dr. G. pointed to the rubble of rocks in a line leading toward the small stream. "That's the Potomac River."

Nac's mouth opened in shock. He looked around again. His eyes went wide. No buildings dotted the horizon. Brown mud was in all directions. In the distance he realized some of the brown clumps must be the remains of buildings as opposed to large boulders like he originally thought.

Nac fell to his knees and caught himself with his fists in the hard brown dirt at his feet. He looked around his former home and audibly sobbed. Dr. G. remained silent. Nac stared ahead. His stomach felt tied in knots. "This can't be right," he mumbled to himself. "How did this happen?"

"We keep agents on long-term missions throughout time. It's similar to the protection missions we had for Marcus when he was younger. They continually upload current events to our central satellite database. I'm downloading their report now. It'll take a few minutes."

Nac stood and removed his clear visor from his pocket and placed it over his eyes. He toggled the view to three hundred percent amplification. He looked in the direction of Congress. A large crater marred the earth. He scanned the entire horizon for any sign of Washington's greatness.

Nothing.

After several minutes Nac finally broke the silence. "We failed."

"Don't be so hasty," Dr. G. firmly replied without hesitation. "I'm starting the download now. It looks like we have data coming in even as of this year. It's a much bigger file than usual."

"That's good, right?" Nac asked.

"It's definitely not a bad thing," Dr. G. replied. The pair looked out over the half-dry dirty gash in the land that marked the Potomac River.

"I think it's a sign of progress," Dr. G. finally concluded.

He paused and checked the download status, still only half complete. "I'm glad you listened to me yesterday."

"What're you talking about?"

Dr. G. smiled. "You're dumber than I remember."

"Careful, everyone isn't here to protect you, this time."

"When I was younger, I attacked Mal that day. He jumped and triggered the car bomb. My auto jump barely saved me. I nearly died on the platform. It took me two years of surgery to recover. Alum stayed with me the entire time. She took care of me, even studying to become a doctor. She still looks after me."

Nac turned and squared his feet to the older man. His eyes squinted.

"One day, you may have to jump back and take over. It'll be up to you to decide if you want to fix my mistakes, or try something new. I'm trying to fix the mistakes I think we made last time, and so far it's working. I know you don't understand yet, but we can't win a head to head fight with the NPs. You'll have to make sacrifices. Everyone on that wall is a friend of mine, or our predecessors."

"So,"

Dr. G. nodded. Nac took a deep breath, exhaling slowly.

"When Diana took care of me, that's when I knew she was the one. She's a fucking unicorn." Dr. G. stated. "Since you don't get the luxury of laying in bed for two years, it's up to you not to fuck it up."

"Hey now, wait a-"

"Do I need to remind you of Tara?"

"No."

"What about Eve? And Erin?

Nac shook his head and looked down.

"How about Victoria, Lauren, and Caroline?"

"Ok, I got it."

"Get rid of the wine you brought back from Marcus'"

"I got it!"

"You better. We don't deserve her. She can't know the truth yet. Alum gets to decide when it's time."

Nac nodded as Dr. G.'s band beeped indicating the download completed. He looked down and quickly analyzed the readouts. Frustration evident in his voice, Dr.G. turned back to Nac. "Large scale conflict gets more likely every day, and the weapons used get deadlier and more destructive. We've delayed the apocalypse. This readout says we bought humanity another hundred years of prosperity. That's nearly four hundred more years since we started the fight.

"However, with each year we gain we also increase the capability to exterminate all life. At the same time tensions are on the rise. Politics, religion, the environment, even simple human migration can be the catalyst to end it all. Individuals trying to better their life, ideologies with harmonious intent, all can spark the chain reaction we've worked so hard to stop. Yet, we keep pushing the timeline back. We keep winning the little battles."

He paused and turned back to the Potomac River.

"Humanity is like a raging river, rushing forward to its own demise. Humans seem to come up with endless new ways for our species to perish. Human nature may be against us, but time is on our side. No matter how strong the river gets, we can build a bigger dam."

"So, now what?" Nac asked.

"We iterate. We keep going. The outcome is inevitable."

Epilogue

As Dr. G. reached down to engage the jump back to headquarters Nac reached out and grabbed his forearm. "What's the craziest shit you've seen?"

"Some AI got out of hand in the Queen City. An augmented reality bear thing required the entire eastern power grid to be shut down to kill it. Texas and the West coast laughed."

"And the dumbest?"

"The 73rd POTUS saw the U.S, and herself, as Noah 2.0."

"Did it work?"

Dr. G. looked at the younger man with scorn. "That iteration was the fastest on record to the end. Once it starts, it almost never stops." He paused and smiled. "You still haven't realized, we're just the North American division. Make sure, when you meet General Fulitz, don't be yourself. Don't poke the bear."

Nac raised an eyebrow. "You know what I'm going to ask?"

"No, but I have a feeling. If I'm right, you'd be two days

earlier than I was, making you right on schedule."

"What do you mean?"

Dr. G. turned and placed a hand on his shoulder. "You can either save them all, or be part of the fight, not both. If you're in, you can only save two; unless you choose Harrison."

Mason Ballowe

// Rolling Paper

// Rolling Paper

// Rolling Paper

// Rolling Paper

About the Author:

Mason Ballowe is a nerd. He holds a Bachelor of Science in Economics from The United States Air Force Academy and a Master of Business Administration from The Darla Moore School Of Business at The University of South Carolina. While completing his service obligation he was awarded the Air Force Achievement Medal for his work with Air Force technology. He is a software engineer, yogi, gamer, lover of The Constitution, and all around good dude. Dr. G. stole his style.

Made in the USA
Columbia, SC
16 September 2019